KNIGHT OF THE SUGAR PLUM FAIRY

ENIGMA SERIES X

TIERNEY JAMES

Publishing Coordinator – Sharon Kizziah-Holmes
Cover Design by Sweet 'N Spicy Designs

L&D PRESS

Owasso, OK

ISBN - 978-1-965460-28-3 (Paperback)
ISBN - 978-1-965460-29-0 (eBook)

DEDICATION

This book is dedicated to the seven little Christmas miracles that are a part of my life 365 days of the year. They are funny, creative, inventive and mischievous, just like Tessa's children in the book. As a matter of fact, they've actually inspired some of the pranks and hilarious shenanigans you read throughout the series where they are concerned. They are my world.

ACKNOWLEDGMENTS

Wizards of Publishing: Much love to my editors Kate Richards and Nan Sipe. You continue to teach and encourage me on each new adventure with the Enigma Team.

Sweet and Spicey Designs: Jayce DeLorenzo never disappoints with her cover designs. She is creative and an excellent listener to what I need.

Paperback Publishing: Sharon Kizziah-Holmes is my major hand holder as she prepares my manuscript for publishing. Anytime I get anxious about a problem with a book she rushes in like a knight in shining armor.

Lipstick and Danger Street Team: Thank you for always giving me your support and encouragement. What would I do without you?

Prologue

Dance-worthy Christmas music played in the background as a man in a hoodie strode out of the woods to join the crowd headed to the Christmas parade in Grass Valley, California. Hundreds of people already found their spot along the streets where the parade would meander through town. Snow flurries gently floated down to land on participants excited at the prospect of a white Christmas.

The man in the hoodie wondered if the entire town might be posing for a Hallmark movie or a tourist brochure. It was perfect. This kind of season and place might also be the perfect cover to blend in while he hunted for the child. People would be too busy with holiday activities, shopping, and maybe snow to notice one more tourist wandering about to enjoy their Cornish Christmas.

The crowds created opportunities for him to slip through and lift unprotected cash from vendor carts where the owner waited on an indecisive customer. A ten-dollar bill wiggled just enough out of a child's pocket as he tried to maneuver his way into Maggie's Toys & Candy Store that the man in the hoodie easily snatched it and moved on. After a trip down one side of the street, he'd collected almost one hundred dollars.

It was enough to purchase a local sweatshirt and a Yuba Gold hat and jacket, all of which he wore out of the store. The shop owner put his old clothes and receipt in a plastic bag for him to carry but paid no more mind to him since others waited their turn to pay for their gifts. He offered a Merry Christmas to the clerk and slipped back outside to hear the pounding drums of a marching band approaching.

How long had it been since he'd celebrated Christmas? Now that he thought about it, he never had. His mother always worked over the school Christmas break, and his father was always drunk. One year after another led him to spending those days in a juvenile detention center, foster care, or on the streets. This had become an opportunity for scoring a lot of cash he didn't have to work very hard to get. Since he'd spotted several police officers patrolling the crowds, he abandoned the thought of acting homeless or blind with a tin cup. Besides, these people were awash in cash to spend for the day, and pickpocketing would be easy enough.

Then he saw her. A father held her up on his shoulders so she could see the marching band coming. How could he know for sure since she left Seattle as a baby? No one knew what she looked like. But this little girl on her daddy's shoulders looked like the mother he left behind.

They were standing in front of an old-time Mercantile store where he knew the little girl's family worked. That much he knew for sure. Several shop personnel, dressed in red aprons and elf hats, came out to enjoy the parade as it passed. He wondered why no one was watching the inside cash registers. But the little girl… Was she the one?

Unexpectantly, he realized her father was staring at him. Even though the father wore aviator sunglasses, he couldn't hide his toughness or the solemn straight line of his mouth. She couldn't be the girl he had to find. The father didn't exactly match the description he'd been given by social services or the nurse who'd helped deliver the child. No matter. She was here somewhere. His friend who had secrets of his own, and wanted to make sure those didn't get repeated, had promised to help.

Then he spotted a familiar man moving through the crowd, trying to look inconspicuous. Didn't matter he wore a ballcap low on his forehead or a camo-style hunting jacket over those stooped shoulders. The walk was slow, and he carried a cane to help with a limp, which was fake. Like himself, he was hiding in plain sight—

another person with a secret. But that secret was more dangerous because the man was a government agent looking for him.

For six weeks, he'd been running away from the agent. Each time, he barely escaped, only to discover his tracks were uncovered once again. He pulled his wallet out to reveal an ID card with the name Anthony Gallo, along with a business card sent to him of a local insurance salesman. He plugged the address into his phone's GPS and decided it was as good a place as any to hide for a few hours. The agent was relentless and had never gotten this close before. Time was running out. He made a mental note: take out FBI agent ASAP.

CHAPTER 1

Captain Chase Hunter stood in the cold waiting for Tessa's kids to finish up their turns acting out the Nativity scene in front of their church. It was too much to hope for that snow blanketing the town would case the seasonal presentation the kids loved and parents pretended to enjoy to be rescheduled. He guessed it was part of the Christmas pageantry of the small town of Grass Valley. Tessa had convinced him to join in the celebration and as usual, it was hard to refuse her.

"Come on. You can be the muscle," Tessa coaxed.

"Why do you need muscle at a Nativity scene? Isn't it about peace on Earth, good will toward men? What could go wrong?" Chase's forehead creased as if he were confused.

"Well, there are live animals. What if they get loose?" she reasoned.

"What kind of animals? Why aren't they cardboard?"

"The children love live animals and they'll come see them and we have a chance to share the good news about Baby Jesus." He knew she started stroking his arm to make him cave. "Do your deacons and Bible-thumper friends know you're a badass who carries a gun and can cut a terrorist off at the knees?" He took a deep breath and let her lean into him. "Nothing says Christmas like—"

"Chase, I think you're missing the point. Just because I've had a few—run-ins with unsavory characters doesn't mean I'm not a good person who wants the world to be a better place." She smiled up at him and, once more, he was a goner. The woman batted those baby blues as if they were a rapid-fire machine gun. "If everyone would embrace the beauty and love of Christmas throughout the year, the world would be a better place."

"Do you hear yourself? How can you preach such nonsense when you know full well, the evil that walks among us?" he huffed.

Tessa wrapped her arms around his tall frame and laid her head against his chest. "Because I believe it can be better. Good trumps evil. You know it's true."

He chuckled as he kissed the top of her head. "I know you are the best thing in my life and I'll do anything to make you happy. Okay. I'll be your muscle. Besides, I'm sure the three ninjas stalking me are probably making plans to embarrass or torment me even as we speak. I will feel better if I keep an eye on them."

"That's the spirit," she cheered, socking a soft fist into his gut. "And don't get distracted when the Ladies Missionary Class brings you cookies or hot chocolate. They're flirting. They think you're a hunk."

"Don't you think I'm a hunk?" he asked, pretending to be bewildered.

"If those ladies knew what you can do in the bedroom, I fear they'd be revoking their baptism and joining Enigma. Just smile and nod when they engage you. I would hate to have to—"

"Say no more." He held up his hand. "I wouldn't want to explain to the police why you sabotaged the good ladies of the church on my behalf."

So, he ended up patrolling the grounds with a couple of other men; one was the chairman of the outreach committee. He heard the man served in Vietnam and the other was a pudgy fellow who resembled a beach ball and sold car insurance. He knew this because he tried his sales pitch on him.

"We're like the Three Musketeers out here, patrolling around the church," the insurance man announced. "Don't you think?"

"Sure," Chase responded drily.

"Or maybe The Three Amigos," the vet named Deacon, mumbled.

"Maybe we should split up," Chase suggested. "I'll go one way, you two go around the back perimeter."

"Military talk. I like that," insurance man admitted as he rubbed his hands together. "Where did you and Tessa meet anyway? You're a lot different from Robert."

"We met at a gun show in Sacramento."

Both men stared at him in surprise.

"She was a babe, and I was on the prowl. The rest is history." Chase let his narrowed gaze go from one man to the other. Finally, they burst into laughter.

"Tessa doesn't fit the profile of a person who would go to a gun show," the insurance man remarked.

"Ha. She is one of those supermoms who hovers like a helicopter. Sweetest lady in the church," Deacon admitted. "Not sure she even lets those rough boys of hers have Nerf guns."

Chase wanted to laugh but kept it under control. He'd taken the boys to a shooting range several times after they went through a hunter safety class and passed with flying colors. Their little sister had shown no interest and demanded he spend time with her on other projects, including a princess tea party with Little Bear and a pony resembling a unicorn, except it was purple and yellow with sparkles on its tail. Painful. But he did it. At least, Tessa was impressed and showed her appreciation later that night when the kids went to stay with their father, Robert Scott.

"Dad thinks you're gay," Sean Patrick announced when he watched out the living room window for Robert.

Chase choked on a sugar cookie Heather had frosted and wanted his opinion on.

"You don't like it," she moaned, sticking out her lip.

He cleared his throat. "No. I mean, yes. It's great." He smiled at Princess Heather with the crown before turning back to the boys. "Why does your dad think I'm gay?" Chase came to stand next to the boy. "What have you been telling him?"

"Not much." Sean Patrick turned to smirk at him. The kid was a walking preteen terrorist to anyone who interfered with his fun. "I may have told him you were always with a bunch of guys from Mom's work, you eat quiche, listen to jazz, and like to cook."

"How does that make me gay?"

"Not my words, big guy. His." He turned his attention to look at Robert Scott pulling up in the circle drive. "Beats me."

Chase had never liked the man and tolerated him, no, kept himself from killing him on a number of occasions. After all, that's what he did for a living most of the time, or it was before he tangled up with the unassuming housewife, Tessa Scott. She'd stumbled into his life with enough innocent chaos to charm a black mamba into being a house pet. Him being the black mamba. They had fought the attraction for several years until her life fell apart and he'd stepped in to be the hero one more time. Robert, the ex-husband, was clueless as to what his wife had gotten herself into, which, if truth be told, was what had ended their marriage.

The kids had no idea how involved he was with their mother. They thought it was a friendship, one without benefits. But he and Tessa had eloped months ago and decided to keep their relationship slow and easy until the kids adjusted to him being around. They liked him, sort of, or pretended to on occasion, except for Heather who was definitely on his side.

And to be honest she had him wrapped around her little finger the moment he laid eyes on her when she was three years old, dressed in a tutu and cowboy boots at the White House. She had the wiles of a twenty-five-year-old starlet, the cunning of a Navy SEAL, and the control of a boss on a chain gang. Her brothers were clueless as to how she manipulated them. It was a bonus she was a great deal like her mother.

Chase reflected back on those moments as he strolled around the church grounds. Tents had been set up with free hot chocolate and cookies for people stopping to listen to carols sung by the choir standing near a blazing bonfire. The church was a few blocks from the main street of Grass Valley where most of the Christmas festivities took place. The church had set up craft booths for children to purchase gifts for family and friends, a clothing donation bin for the homeless, a food pantry if there was a need, and an opportunity to bring a shoebox with goodies to send to the children of third world countries in time for Christmas. If you were hungry, the church provided a chili supper served inside the recreation hall for a three-dollar donation. If you couldn't afford it, then donate whatever you could, even if it was a smile and a thank-you.

He had to admit, the outreach impressed him. The congregation appeared to be enjoying themselves, along with a number of people stopping by. Whether it was the live Nativity Scene, or the cuteness of the children acting out their parts, there was always a crowd gathered to watch. Once the donkey brayed so loud, none of the words were heard, but the applause indicated the onlookers were entertained nonetheless.

When he made the rounds, he took a few extra minutes to check out the Nativity scene. Where were Tessa's kids were character actors.

"I'm Mary," bragged Heather and raised her chin in self-confidence before they left the house. "I'm going to rock this part."

"I bet you will." Chase grinned and pinched her cheek. "Daniel, what is your part?"

"I wanted to play one of the Three Wise Men because they always look cool on Christmas cards. But the older boys got those parts. I'm a shepherd. I look up at the sky and say something about the heavenly host, I think."

"Don't you know your part yet?" Chase quizzed.

He shrugged. "As long as I'm holding the lamb, nobody is going to care. They'll be thinking how cute I am."

"Hopefully, it won't poop on you." Sean Patrick smirked.

"And what part do you play?" he quizzed the oldest.

"I wanted to play King Herod."

Chase sighed. "Of course, you did. I'm not surprised." He pinched the top of his nose in frustration. "And why is that, Sean Patrick?"

"Well, he was the guy with all the power."

"Yeah, I'm thinking that takes a turn for the worse as time goes on," Chase reminded him.

The boy frowned. "Oh yeah. Forgot about that. Too late now. I'm committed."

"Which I will be if I survive this Christmas festival," he mumbled. Folding his arms across his chest and with his feet slightly apart, he wondered if he had taken on the appearance of an angry drill segreant. With his stocking cap pulled a little farther down on his forehead than normal, he figured it intimidated several visitors, considering they gave him a wide berth.

"You know you look like you just escaped prison, right? Would it hurt you to wear something festive?" Tessa had teased before they all piled into the car and headed to the church. "I mean, I love this look, but some of my friends might—"

"Your friends will be eyeballing me like a pack of hyenas over a fresh lion kill."

Her laughter made him want to kiss her right there in the car, but the kids were watching every move he made of late. Instead, he reached over, laid his hand on hers, and squeezed. She handed him a pair of reindeer antlers with flashing red lights twinkling on and off when a button on the back was touched.

"Oh, Chasey! You've got to wear them. Please. Please. Please," Heather chirped. "For me."

He turned to check to see if she was buckled into her car seat. "No way. Soldiers don't wear antlers, not even for a princess." She stuck out a quivering lip and batted her eyelashes like Tessa did when she lied. Only, this time, he thought tears would soon follow as she bowed her head in disappointment. "Well, maybe I could for a few minutes if you'll come walk with me after you finish your part in the play," he coaxed.

She jerked her head up and grinned as she held out her hand to her brothers. "Told you! Hand it over," she ordered.

The boys handed over a candy stash they pulled from their pockets.

"What just happened?" he demanded.

Heather put the candy in her cupholder. "They bet I couldn't get you to agree to wear the antlers. I was pretty sure I could."

He was pretty sure the halo he imagined circling her head became a bit more tarnished. Then she blew him a kiss, and he moaned as he turned back to Tessa who was struggling not to laugh out loud.

"Did you know about this? Why am I asking you? You'll just lie." He adjusted the mirror to see the boys. "And you two. What happened to guys stick together? No soldier left behind and all that you're always spouting to me? Huh?"

Daniel pushed his glasses up on his nose with his middle finger extended. Chase wasn't sure he did it on purpose. "It was a social experiment. We stick together from now on."

"Glad to hear it because"—Chase reached under the seat and

pulled out a plastic bag then tossed it over his shoulder—"you'll be on patrol with me later, and I want you to wear these."

The boys pulled out two striped hats with large elf ears. "You can't be serious," Sean Patrick snarled.

Chase turned on the ignition and leveled a dangerous glare toward the boys, causing them to sit a little straighter in their seats. "We'll see how the evening goes. No mischief tonight."

"No problem, sir," Sean Patrick offered in the military voice he used to gain traction and respect from him.

Chase arched an eyebrow and frowned. "I'm counting on it, gentlemen."

That, of course, flew out the window without a second thought.

CHAPTER 2

Chase felt a prickle at the nape of his neck similar to when he was in Afghanistan. His body stiffened as his arms fell to his side. The only things that moved were his eyes, searching out trouble.

What did he see? Mostly a lot of folks strolling around carrying cups of hot chocolate. Others mouthed words that formed breathy clouds followed by the light laughter he'd come to understand normal people shared this time of year. It was yet another thing he needed to learn to fit into Tessa's world.

What did he feel? The cold seeping through his gloves made his trigger finger twitch. This, too, occurred when his hypersensitivity to the environment kicked in. The joy others appeared to experience here made him uneasy. He shifted his weight to take in the surrounding area in one glance. All this joy, peace on earth, good will toward men felt like a good way to spring a sneak attack while everyone's guard was down. This was too trusting and lackadaisical for his warrior's heart.

What did he hear? He raised his chin at the sound of a familiar shepherd's voice. Daniel appeared at the corner of the prayer garden where King Herod, taking a break from the Nativity play, was making snow boobs on the resident angel that watched over the place of reflection and tranquility. Sean Patrick still wore the robes of the king as he managed to shape a bikini brief on the poor heavenly creature, making her look like a stripper. With a devilish smirk on his face, he grabbed Daniel's shepherd's staff and tried to place it in front of the angel to make the scene complete. But he hesitated when Daniel jabbered anxiously with concerns Chase couldn't make out.

Whatever the younger boy was animated about ended with him waving back toward the Nativity set. Sean Patrick kicked up a clump of snow. At first, Chase thought the kid would clobber his younger brother in anger. Instead, he twirled the staff like he was Bruce Lee. Daniel ran and motioned for big brother to follow, which he did in slow, angry stomps.

"That can't be good."

What did he smell? Smoke? He turned his head around to see the bonfire where several ladies were helping children make s'mores. No. It was more than that. He sniffed as he stepped toward where he'd seen the boys disappear. Smoke, a shepherd's staff, and boys were not a good combination, especially those two boys.

Then he realized Deacon Monroe had fallen into step beside him. "Smell that?"

Chase nodded and picked up speed until he found himself running and reached the Nativity. It took a second for him to spot Sean Patrick and another boy wrestling on the ground, throwing punches like they were part of the World Wrestling Federation. Daniel knelt by Heather next to another little girl who sobbed uncontrollably. Both girls were covered in snow. Heather was hugging her while Daniel knocked the snow off their faces and clothes.

"What the hell?" Chase mumbled.

The yellow flash of fire sprang up in the corral where the animals were running in circles. The two donkeys braying slammed against the railing, trying to escape. The steer followed the donkeys, and the pigmy pig let a squeal that would have awakened the dead. The adjoining pen held two saddled camels the children had been riding with their handlers leading them around the grounds earlier. They were being nervously led out of confinement only to jerk free and head out toward the street.

Other men joined the chaos and, together, they managed to

flip over the water trough to slow down the advancement of flames.

"Deacon, get the girls," Chase ordered as he stormed toward the boys. Lifting Sean Patrick up by the back of the collar revealed Pastor Paxton's son, with a bloody nose, and what most likely would be a doozy of a black eye. The boy also had a head full of snow and even more filling the top of his coat.

Without releasing Sean Patrick, Chase reached down and grabbed the front of the boy's coat and pulled him to his feet. He was a head taller than Sean Patrick and about twenty pounds heavier. The two had a history of not getting along. When the boy became aware of who had intervened, he grabbed Chase's arm with both hands.

"C-Captain Hunter," he stammered. "It was an accident."

The sound of fire trucks and loud voices, mixed with the red strobe lights flooded the once-serene image of Christmas past. Firefighters let go a cannon blast of water toward the Nativity lean-to, sending the baby Jesus into a nearby tree and splintering the manger into a lopsided pile of kindling.

Pastor Paxton ran into the chaos, trying to calm nervous moms and telling a few of the dads to stop using the Lord's name in vain, before joining Chase. He released the larger boy to the care of his father who eyeballed his son with skepticism and disappointment. While glancing at his wild bunch to make sure Heather, Daniel, and the other little girl were safe, Chase saw Tessa lift her daughter in her arms. Deacon knelt then scooped up the little girl he knew as Kelly. The two girls reached out to each other and held hands until Kelly's parents gathered her into grateful arms with lots of kisses to her chubby cheeks.

Tessa and Daniel moved toward him as he continued to grip Sean Patrick's collar with an iron fist. Sean Patrick was still tense and flushed with rage as he tried to step toward the Paxton boy, only to be jerked against Chase's body.

"Sean Patrick." Tessa's voice reminded Chase of his friend Zoric's tone seconds before he waterboarded a terrorist. "Young man, I certainly hope you can explain this."

"Yes, ma'am. I can." The boy had retreated to a military voice that worked like a magic potion on his mother. If he hadn't, the mild-mannered, cookie-baking, kick-ass mother would make his life miserable. He admitted to feeling a little sorry for the kid as a chill ran up his spine.

Mrs. Paxton ran to the group and pushed in front of her husband, gathering her son into her arms. “Oh my,” she wailed then turned toward Sean Patrick. “I guess all this is because of you,” she accused.

“Now, hold on, Ellen,” Tessa spoke softly. Chase knew that tone, too. He was trying to remember if she had a knife in her coat pocket. “We don’t know what happened. I’m sure there are no innocent parties here.”

Heather shook her finger at the Paxton boy. “He was smoking a cigarette.”

Ellen gasped. “Don’t be ridiculous.”

Tessa handed Heather to Chase’s free arm. He had to release her son to keep from dropping the little girl.

“Excuse me?” She took a breath and exhaled slowly. Enigma training had been good for her. “Let’s just calm down,” Tessa continued patiently.

“If there is trouble, mayhem, or bullying, you’ll find Sean Patrick,” Ellen snapped. “If you took care of—”

Pastor Paxton finally spoke up. “That’s enough, Ellen. Hush.”

“Humph,” she snapped as she grabbed her son’s hand and tried to pass Tessa.

Very casually, Tessa stuck out her foot, tripping Ellen so that she fell face-first into a snowbank. “Oh my gosh.” Tessa scrambled to help the woman. As she caught the woman’s arm and Ellen tried to stand, Tessa released her so she fell in the snow a second time. “Oops.”

Chase set Heather down and helped Pastor Paxton with Ellen. She spit snow, making her son laugh, which caused his mother to storm off angrily. “Go with your mother, son.”

“I’m very sorry, Pastor Paxton.” Tessa batted those baby blues as Chase leveled a dangerous glare at her.

“I’m sure you are,” he confessed. “I see the police are here. I’m guessing we’ll have a great deal of explaining to do. Don’t go far.”

When the pastor had moved out of earshot, Chase glanced at Tessa. “You totally did that on purpose.”

“Mom? What does Chasey mean?” Heather asked sweetly.

"There's Officer Michaels. He doesn't look happy. Sean Patrick, tell the truth." Chase extended his hand to the police officer who had helped him foil an attempt on his life one Christmas. "Well look who it is." The officer tried his best to sound friendly.

"I should have known your bunch would be behind a little friendly chaos." He turned to Tessa and gave a half smile. "I'm going to have to talk to your son as soon as we get the animals rounded up. I passed two camels headed down the hill toward Main Street. As to these other animals, looks like several have been injured. Vets have been called in to check them over. If you'll wait inside, I won't be long."

"Are you taking my brother to jail?" Heather's voice turned a little shaky.

Fortunate for him, Kelly ran up and hugged Sean Patrick as if her life depended on it. Chase watched the boy reach down and pat her cheeks as she smiled up at him. That's when he noticed the little girl had Down syndrome.

"I wuv you, Sean Patrick."

"You'd better." He smiled bigger than Chase had ever seen him do.

The police officer arched his eyebrows. "I have a feeling there is a lot more to this story than two boys fighting."

Kelly's parents came up and thanked Sean Patrick for watching after their daughter. He shifted from foot to foot and stared down at the ground then up at Chase who reached out and put a hand on the boy's shoulder as Tessa smiled at her oldest.

Chase was wondering how he got lucky enough to be a part of this family, when Tessa rose on her tiptoe and whispered in his ear, "Divine intervention."

CHAPTER 3

The ride home could have passed for a mission carried out by a Stealth Bomber. Chase had instructed the boys to buckle up in the back seat of Tessa's SUV as he carried Heather around to her seat on the opposite side. He carefully fastened her belts and tried to withdraw, but her little hands touched his face, freezing him in place. Those eyes bored into his soul as she smiled and pulled him forward to kiss his cheek. Without thinking, he kissed her back and tucked a curl under her hat. Then he slid a narrowed gaze toward the boys who stared straight ahead as if they'd turned into a block of salt like Lot's wife in the Bible after disobeying God.

Where was God when you needed an identical reprimand with two rambunctious boys? Such a concept would certainly make his life easier. For a few seconds, he tried to envision the possibilities.

He'd turned on the ignition of the car when he noticed Tessa stomping across the open space between the church and parking lot. Her head was down and her hands doubled into fists. Adjusting the rearview mirror to see the boys, he watched Sean Patrick elbow his brother and nod toward their mother. Daniel rolled his eyes and shook his head as if he knew a storm was about to hit.

But it didn't. Chase had to admit, her silence created a bigger impact than exploding all at once. Let the little rascals stew in their own mischief for a while. All she said was, "Take us home." The calm in her voice managed to unnerve him. After seeing the woman spray a bunch of terrorists with an AR-15 in Syria, he wasn't going to underestimate her ability to scare the hell out of anyone.

A light snow fell, slowing their progress. Chase put the vehicle in four-wheel drive and proceeded with caution. This gave him time to piece together the events of the last couple of hours and rehash the police interview. The face of Kelly when she hugged Sean Patrick was his first clue he had jumped in for a rescue.

The Grass Valley fire and rescue department had extinguished the fire in a matter of a few minutes, but it appeared the live Nativity would need a miracle to continue in the coming days. All the animals had been rounded up. The camels had led the police department on a slippery chase with little success until a local rancher worked with the owners to lasso them. With gentle coaxing, and a great deal of camel spit expelled in rebellion, they, too, returned to the scene of the crime. Then they were loaded onto a truck and taken back to their home down in the valley.

Officer Michaels was sweating when he came inside the church recreation room where potlucks, baby showers, and game nights were hosted. The kitchen squad was making their final cleanup for the night, offering the boys and their parents the last of the sugar cookies. Chase leveled a dangerous warning at his bunch.

"No thank you, Mrs. Jones." Sean Patrick held up his hand in refusal. "We've probably had enough sugar. Mom doesn't approve of us having too much. Not healthy, you know."

The gray-haired lady reached out and patted his cheek. "Well, aren't you the sweetest thing to listen to your momma like that?"

"Yes, ma'am."

She leaned in toward Chase. "That kid is a menace. Whatever Sean Patrick did to him, I'm sure he deserved it."

Chase spotted a smirky grin on Sean's face as if he'd won a few points. "Yes. He's quite the boy." He smiled at the lady. "I'll take one of those cookies. I heard these were the best in town."

"Why, I made those myself," she cooed.

"You are an artist, dear lady. Thank you." Chase could turn on the charm and had done so many times to get what he wanted. He took a bite and rolled his eyes upward. "Pure heaven."

She giggled and walked away as Tessa came to sit down beside him. "Are you flirting with Mrs. Jones?"

"Yes. You'd better get this recipe or I'm trading up. Your position for being my number one is in jeopardy." When she smiled seductively and arched an eyebrow, he choked on the cookie. "I can be persuaded, however."

"You're weak, Captain Hunter."

"Happily, so, I might add."

Officer Michaels pulled up a chair and removed his hat before running his fingers through his short hair. "Well, this has been a night. I've been visiting with Kelly's parents." He took out a notebook and ran his fingers down the page. "Wanted to see what your side of the story is." He eyeballed the three Scott children then focused on their mother. "Is that okay with you, Tessa?"

They were on a first-name basis after the Christmas fiasco a couple of years earlier. She was known to bake him and his fellow officers a batch of her chocolate chip cookies at least once a month to show appreciation for their hard work. They loved it and always enjoyed hearing the naughty shenanigans the kids had been up to.

She agreed and slipped her arm onto the back of Sean Patrick's chair. He wondered if it was to be able to lay a hand on his shoulder and give a little squeeze if she detected the beginning of a twisted version of the truth. From the solemn expression on her face, chances were good she already knew the whole story. Whether she was angry, amused, or frustrated was yet to be discovered. In normal circumstances, he could read her expressions as to whether she was scared, confused, or lying. But, when it came to her kids and discipline, the woman could have been a straight-faced poker player in Vegas.

"Who wants to go first?" the officer asked with a friendly grin. "Heather, how about you?"

"Is Kelly okay?" she asked anxiously.

"Yep. Just talked to her mom and dad. They're on their way home. It was a lot of excitement for you two fine ladies."

She smiled shyly and shook her head quickly. "Kelly and I were looking at the animals."

Daniel butted in. "I was with them. Mom said not to let Heather be alone with so many people around."

"Your mom is very wise," Officer Michaels added.

Daniel shifted his attention to Sean Patrick then frowned. "My brother left. He was supposed to help me when our parts were over at the Nativity. But did he? No." He folded his arms high on his chest resembling an angry Buddha.

When the officer glanced at Sean, he shrugged nonchalantly. "I forgot."

"Liar," Daniel accused.

Tessa's hand went to the back of Sean Patrick's head and touched his hair.

"What I meant was, I thought since Daniel was there, I'd go get us hot chocolate." He turned to his mom. "I was so cold playing the part in the Nativity. I figured Daniel and Heather were, too. I wanted to help them out. You know, because I'm the oldest."

"Oh yeah? How were you going to carry three cups of hot chocolate?" Daniel snapped. "What you said was 'I'll be back,' like that Terminator character."

"Anyway." Tessa snapped her fingers. "Then what happened?"

Her hand was now on Sean's shoulder and might have been massaging his collarbone or injecting a kind of truth serum with her perfectly manicured nails. Chase was betting on the latter when he reached around Tessa and soft bumped the kid's knee with his fist.

"It's okay, buddy. Just tell the truth."

Sean Patrick sighed. "I did slip away to get hot chocolate for myself, but I didn't get far. Next thing I knew, Daniel was running up to me. I was mad because Heather wasn't with him. That's when he told me Luther was picking on the girls."

Daniel unfolded his arms. "More like bullying. Luther lit up a cigarette, and I told him to stop because there was hay." He blushed. "He shoved me backward and told me I was a wuss."

Heather nodded vehemently; lips pooched out. "So, I said, 'Leave my brother alone.' "

The officer appeared to be fighting back a grin. "Then what happened?"

"He shoved my sister. That made me mad, and I kicked him," Daniel said.

About this time, Sean Patrick groaned as if his brother had just thrown the championship for a wrestling match.

"Well, Sean, he's a lot bigger than me. I had to use what I had. Right, Chase?"

Chase gave him a thumbs-up with pride. "Right, buddy. Probably a good decision. Glad you were taking up for your sister."

Heather stuck her bottom lip out farther as she spoke. "Then Kelly ran to help Daniel, and Luther laughed and called her a retard."

A heavy silence fell on the adults. Chase had the urge to go get the kid and give him a good old-fashioned come-to-Jesus talk that involved a switch across the butt like he'd gotten a few times as a mischievous preteen. But parents didn't approve of those discipline techniques anymore.

"He called her lots of names, Mom." Daniel's face distorted, as if he were hurting. "She's such a sweet kid. She only wanted to help me. I tried to protect the girls but…but…I couldn't." He lowered his gaze to his feet. "He shoved the girls down in the snow and hit their faces with snowballs. Hard ones. I knew I needed help."

"That's when he came for me," Sean Patrick offered matter-of-factly. "When I saw the girls, I lost it. Luther threw his cigarette down and, well, I guess it was in some dry hay. You pretty much know the rest. Am I going to jail for arson?"

Officer Michaels brow creased, and his bottom lip jutted in and out. "Nope."

"Assault and battery?"

"Probably not."

"Disturbing the peace?"

"Well, that's a possibility, I guess. Those runaway camels did stir up a lot of chaos."

"I'm sorry about the camels and the Nativity scene catching fire, but I'm not sorry for beating the holy crap out of Luther. He's such a—"

"What Sean Patrick means is Luther tends to pick on these kids at every opportunity," Chase interjected, afraid of what might be coming out of the kid's mouth next.

"Yeah. What he said." Sean nodded toward Chase. "If Luther says otherwise, he's a big fat liar." Sean's tone would have frozen water on a summer day in Death Valley.

The officer gave Sean Patrick a hard stare before he shifted his attention to Chase and Tessa. “We need to talk about this at some point—without the kids.”

“Maybe I should take the kids to the car.” Chase stood and motioned for the kids to follow him.

“Thanks, Chase.” Tessa’s gaze showed a fleeting expression of helplessness.

It wasn’t easy being a single parent. The father of these rascals, Robert, wasn’t much help in these matters. Learning when to step in to take over a situation with these kinds of matters was still new to Chase. He vowed to be there for her and the kids. Sean Patrick was already a handful and required guidance from a man. This might be one of those times to step back a little to see how things played out.

Heather wiggled out of her folding chair in quick order. She smiled up at him then grabbed his hand and squeezed. “Let’s go, Chasey.”

He bent down and whispered, “I asked you not to call me that.”

She covered her mouth, eyes widened in surprise. “Okay. Let’s go, Dad. How’s that?” Leaning into him, she wrapped her arms around his lowered body and hugged him.

Chase felt the familiar pain in his chest he used to get when Tessa walked into a room and smiled at him. No two ways about it. He was a goner when it came to Heather and her mother. “I think I love you, Heather,” he said, swinging her up in his arms. “Now let’s blow this Popsicle stand.”

She gave him a thumbs-up, followed by a giggle. The boys were already waiting at the door, anxious to be out of harm’s way.

Now he glanced at Tessa who stared, deep in thought, out the windshield. There had been no hiding her anger when she’d gotten in the car. Those blue eyes had turned a shade of violet he’d seen on occasion when she got riled. Most of the time, he found it intriguing, but now kids were involved. He was anxious to see how this would play out.

The moment of reckoning was on the horizon.

Special FBI Agent Dennis Martin had been in town over a

week. The trail of Anthony Gallo had gone cold, once again, after the debacle in Seattle. He had been first on the scene in North Carolina after the transfer of Gallo turned into a monumental disaster. The transfer was to take place in a police station in Raleigh, North Carolina. Due to a college professor's call for anarchy to take the police state, the decision was made to relocate the handoff. At the last minute, the rendezvous was changed to Pullen Park near the statue of Andy Griffith and Ron Howard who starred in the Andy Griffith TV show.

Murphy's law, "If anything can go wrong, it will go wrong," decided to play a joke on the state troopers who stopped at a railroad crossing with a train across the tracks. It was carrying a load of lumber that shifted and caused the twenty shipping containers to derail. One slid toward the waiting vehicles, the troopers' transport van being second in line. The rolling container shoved the nearest vehicle into the troopers' and flipped it over. When the troopers revived, Anthony Gallo was gone.

Now, here he was in Grass Valley. Not a feel-good place to be, since it was heavy with the smell of Enigma agents who always felt like he owed them a favor. He stayed under the radar while looking for Gallo. With any luck, he'd catch the dangerous felon and have him back where he belonged. He decided against notifying the local police, since, in his opinion, they'd go all cowboy and screw things up, causing Gallo to hightail it to Mexico. He realized now, that may have been a mistake.

When the fire engines turned the tranquil calm to chaos, he watched people rush toward the fire on the hill. He took the back way to beat the crowds. He moved among the crowd, suspecting Gallo might show up at such a function since there would be a lot families present. Mostly, he wondered if the man hadn't started the fire as a diversion. Things calmed down pretty fast and first responders and ambulances finished up their duties as the agent decided this had been a lost cause. Then as luck would have it, he spotted someone who matched Gallo's description watching kids getting into an SUV with a familiar Enigma agent. When he saw Tessa walking across the grounds, dodging a couple of police officers, he determined Gallo had been watching the Scott children. The felon was here to pick up a girl. What if he kidnapped the wrong one?

Cautiously, he exited the car, pulled his weapon, and approached. The shadowy figure turned and spotted him. The strobe lights of first responder vehicles highlighted his face.

"Down on the ground, Gallo," he ordered.

In that instant, an ambulance gurney pushed passed him, causing him to take his eyes off Gallo who took off running through the crowd. The agent followed, only to watch the escapee jump into a beat-up pickup truck and head out of the parking lot. By the time he got back to his own vehicle and tried to follow, he thought he'd lost him. Spotting him swerving up the Summer Berry Hill Road, he increased his speed. To his surprise, Gallo managed to turn the truck around and sped toward him. The agent swerved and crashed into the rock columns of a gated community. He recognized the name of the subdivision on the sign, now hanging lopsided on the column. As blood spilled from a cut somewhere over his eye, he fought the airbag, realizing Gallo was trying to send him a message: he'd found his child. Heather Scott.

CHAPTER 4

Chase pulled into the garage with the click of seat belt unbuckling at the same time. Heather's chirpy voice sang "Silent Night" mixed with "Jingle Bell Rock." There were a few moments when he was confused at which was which with her new version. The boys silently escaped the car while their mother helped Heather out of her car seat. Chase entered the house and once more was taken aback at the romanticized decorations Tessa had created for Christmas. He hoped they would brighten her mood.

"How about a cup of hot tea?" he offered as they hung up coats and hats in the entryway off the garage.

"Decaf."

He nodded and headed toward the kitchen with children shoving past him, followed by thundering footsteps up the walnut staircase. This was all so new to him. Usually when he came home from an Enigma mission, he retreated to his condo in Sacramento where quiet reigned supreme. That kind of peace was absent here. Once more, he wondered how Tessa had managed to keep her wits about her these last few years with such chaos spinning around her after returning home from danger.

"Are you okay?" He handed her a mug of hot tea.

"Yes. Thank goodness you were there to help." She held her

cup with both hands, letting its warmth seep through her fingers. When her hand trembled, he took the tea and set it on the counter.

"Come here." He pulled her into his arms. "You should be proud of the boys for trying to save the day."

"They could have been hurt if the fire had reached them. And the girls…"

"But I was there and, besides the missing baby Jesus, I think everything else turned out okay." He chuckled. "That doll shot out of the manger like a shoulder-held rocket-launcher when the fire department hit it with a blast of water."

"After you took the kids to the car, Ellen Paxton insinuated I was a bad mom and this was my fault."

He rubbed her back gently then backed up to sit on the barstool. "What did I miss?"

"Luther told Officer Michaels it was Daniel who tried to smoke then handed it to him." She huffed and threw up her hands. "Can you imagine Daniel doing such a thing?"

"Yes. Actually, I can."

"What?" she fumed.

"Boys try all kinds of crap when they're young, Tessa. It's in our DNA."

"That's nonsense. I've never even taken a puff of a cigarette. I took my first sip of wine when I was twenty-six."

"Yes. And you were a virgin when you got married," he reminded her. "Your only fault is you believe you're perfect."

Heather slid into the kitchen in her footie pajamas and hugged her mom's legs before climbing up on a stool next to Chase. "Virgin? Chasey. Oops. Sorry. This guy knows all about virgins. He told me everything I need to know," she spoke matter-of-factly.

"Is that so?" Tessa's eyes began to change color again.

He held up his hand. "It's not what you think," Chase rushed to explain. "I told the kids the history of the song 'Silent Night.' Heather had questions."

Tessa's eyes were pure violet now.

"I-I just said it was— Honestly, I don't know what I said, but not what you think."

"Mommy, were you a virgin when Sean Patrick was born?"

"No, baby girl."

"Why not?"

"It's complicated."

"I think that's what Chasey said, too. Will I be a virgin when I have a baby?"

"Oh Lord," she moaned. "I'm not ready for this conversation."

"Don't worry about it, Mommy. Sean Patrick says he knows all about it, and any time I have questions, I can come to him. Do you want him to talk to you, too?"

Chase had to bite the inside of his mouth to keep from bursting into laughter.

The expression on Tessa's face had morphed from angry to terrified. "Number one: you scoot along, and I'll tuck you in soon. Number two: if you have more questions, you come to me for answers, not Sean. Number three: I would very much like to talk to Sean Patrick, so send him down ASAP."

The little girl pushed off the stool and put her hands on her hips as she addressed Chase. "That means he better hurry or his ass is grass."

Tessa sucked in her breath in horror. "Young lady, you watch your mouth. We don't talk like that in this house."

Heather's bottom lip pushed out, and she looked down at the floor. "Sorry, Mommy."

"Give me a kiss then off to bed." Tessa reached for her, but she turned to Chase and motioned for him to bend down. Once he was at eye level, she kissed his cheek. "You'll get your kiss when you tuck me in, Mommy." She lifted an accusing finger to her mother.

Tessa poked Chase and smiled as he watched her escape. Chase shook his head and pinched the top of his nose with his finger. "I'm a goner with that one. I'm laying the law down right now. No boyfriends, dates, or social media until she's twenty-five. Are we clear?"

Tessa arched an eyebrow. "Good luck. Like mother like daughter."

Sean Patrick strolled into the kitchen, head held high, sporting St. Louis Cardinal pajamas. Chase was a Giants fan and thought maybe he'd get the kid those pajamas for Christmas. Hopefully, he'd be rebellious enough he'd wear them to irritate his mother.

"Yes, ma'am?" Her steely-eyed appraisal locked on him. Only his fingers twitched in anticipation of a reprimand. Chase had to admit the kid had guts.

Tessa motioned for him to come closer. He did without hesitation. “I wanted you to know how proud I am of you. What you did tonight, although risky, was a brave thing to do for the girls.” She put a hand on each of his forearms, and he fell against her so she could hold him tight. “I love you tons, Sean Patrick.”

“I didn’t mean to embarrass you, Mom.”

“You didn’t. But I’m afraid there are consequences for your actions.”

“Jail?”

“No. You’ll have to go help with repairs tomorrow and work tomorrow night for both play presentations. You’ll have to clean up after the animals, as well, so the grounds will look nice for Sunday services.”

He tried to nod his head in agreement even though it was against her shoulder. The kid was a bit taller than his mother.

“And you’ll have to donate your money from mowing lawns to buy supplies for repairs.”

“But—”

“No buts, Sean Patrick.”

“Yes, ma’am,” he moaned. He stepped back and glanced at Chase. “Thanks for not killing me.”

“You’re welcome,” Chase offered flatly. It was difficult not to give the kid a high five for being a hero to the girls.

“Give your mom a kiss and off to bed.” She tried her best to kiss him on each cheek, but he squirmed away.

“Mom,” he fumed. He rubbed the kiss away. “I’m too old for that mushy stuff.”

“Which reminds me. If Heather has any questions about the birds and the bees—”

“I don’t know anything about animals or insects. Why would I tell her about that?”

Tessa sighed and then held her breath for a few seconds. “I know you know what I’m talking about. If your sister asks you about sex, then you send her to me.”

Chase came to stand next to Tessa. “And if you have any questions, then you come to me.”

The boy’s eyes glazed over as he eyed Chase and shifted his attention back to Tessa. “Got it. No sex talk to the kid, and White

Knight here will give me a lecture on protection." Sean Patrick backed out as Tessa gasped and covered her mouth. "What? I was talking about self-defense, Mom. What did you think I was talking about?"

Tessa's shoulder's slumped in relief. "That. Yeah. Self-defense. Go." She turned away and missed Sean Patrick locking gazes with Chase then giving a thumbs-up.

Chase mouthed the words, "We'll talk later."

Tessa took a sip of the now-cold tea and decided to warm it in the microwave. After retrieving the cup after the ding, she turned to Chase. "You were saying something about male DNA, mischievous boys, I think."

"I think Luther is lying to save his own skin. He's Pastor Paxton's kid after all. You know how they talk about pastor and missionary kids. I know firsthand. Even though my parents were missionary doctors in China, I was a handful. The Chinese are probably still looking for me." He laughed. "Not excusing the brat, but I've been there."

She took a deep breath. "Since tomorrow is Saturday, the men of the church said they'd make repairs. The camels won't return for tomorrow night's program, but the small animal farmer said he'd be happy to bring a pony and a few rabbits, maybe a calf and pot-bellied pig."

"And baby Jesus?"

"One of the firemen used the water to knock it out of the tree, but unfortunately the head is now MIA. We can take one of Heather's dolls."

The doorbell rang, and both moved toward the front door.

"Kinda late for visitors," Chase admitted. "Expecting anyone?"

Tessa frowned and shook her head.

Filled with an overabundance of caution, Chase used the peephole to see who was outside. He jerked the door open, and FBI Agent Dennis Martin staggered inside, covered in blood. "Ho. Ho. Ho." He proceeded to fall unconscious into Chase's outstretched arms.

CHAPTER 5

Paramedics and the police soon followed, dimming the solar Christmas lights wrapped around every tree and bush that outlined Tessa's house. Emergency vehicles filled her circular driveway. When the fire truck pulled up, her kids came thundering down to join in the fray.

Rather than be concerned about the FBI agent bleeding on her new Christmas rug in the foyer, all she could think about was One: I'm never going to get those kids to sleep now. Two: if their father gets wind of this, she'll have a lot of explaining to do as to why Agent Martin selected her house in which to collapse. Three: the ex would want to know why Chase Hunter was at her house at such a late hour.

Fortunately, the paramedics administered first aid, and Agent Martin quickly roused, dazed but lucid enough to be his cantankerous self, especially when he saw three kids eyeballing him. There was a definite snarl on his lips and a two-inch cut above his eyebrow. With a bruise on his cheek, a knot above the cut, and a puddle of melted snow clinging to his black trench coat, he resembled a person who might require a pair of handcuffs for a fashion statement.

"You kids should go to bed," Chase growled as he assisted

Agent Martin to a chair. When they didn't move, he jerked his head toward the stairs.

"Is everything all right, Mommy?" asked Heather with a face laced with anxiety.

Tessa scooped her up into her arms and landed a short kiss on her nose. "Yes. This is an old friend, and looks like he may have had a car accident down the street. Getting slick outside. Got a nasty bump on his head. Now, you run along. I'll be up when I can."

"Why was he coming here?" Sean Patrick inquired as he put his hands on his hips.

"Yeah. And how do you know him?" Daniel added.

"Those are really good questions, boys. I can't answer them right now, so scoot."

"But—" Sean Patrick protested until Chase slowly stood up and leveled a dangerous glare his way. This sent all three scurrying up the steps and to their rooms.

Tessa felt a little amused, in spite of Agent Martin's predicament. She loved the way Chase could control a situation with those black eyes of his. They sent chills up her spine and not in a bad way.

The first responders began to leave since Agent Martin had refused further treatment. Her favorite local police officer remained.

"Why is it, Tessa, your family has such an interesting life?"

"Officer Michaels, I have no idea what you mean. We are just like everyone else in the neighborhood."

He burst out laughing and pulled out a chair without asking and sat down. "You crack me up. And you"—he pointed to Chase—"I know you're big-time trouble. Now, this guy shows up on your doorstep after being on a slip-and-slide. And"—he flipped open a two-sided passport book that held Agent Martin's badge and identification credentials then returned it to him—"he turns out to be FBI with a crashed car at the subdivision gate, which he manages to get out of and somehow walks here with a busted head. I'm definitely putting in for overtime. Hell, I'll work this case even if I have to do it for free."

"There's no case," Agent Martin said, accepting an ice pack from Tessa.

The officer smirked. “Right.” He slowly cut his eyes to Tessa. “I guess Agent Martin maybe came for romantic reasons?”

Agent Martin grimaced. “That’s right. I’ve got this thing for obnoxious women with three kids who most likely have wanted posters at the post office.”

“Excuse me,” Tessa snapped. “I have you know they were never convicted, and those posters have been removed.”

Chase rubbed his hand across his face and shook his head. “Officer Michaels, what exactly do you want to know? If you stay much longer, I’m afraid Tessa might decide to spank you.”

“As tempting as that sounds, I just need to know what is going on. Was this really just an accident, or is something more sinister going on?”

“This is a need-to-know event, and you’re not on the list.” Agent Martin moaned as he touched the knot on his forehead. “Tessa, do you have any coffee?”

“No.” She folded her arms across her chest. “Besides, I thought you retired or something.”

“I thought he got fired after that little incident of stealing a snowplow a couple of Christmases ago,” Chase added.

“That was to protect your once-psycho girlfriend from Ireland and your current Miss Sunshine who is bound to suck the mean right out of you.”

“That psycho girlfriend from Ireland is now my best friend, so watch yourself,” Tessa said sweetly.

“Figures. Ying and yang. Chase, I never thought you one for playing with fire.” Agent Martin twisted his mouth in a lopsided grin.

Officer Michaels held up both his hands. “As entertaining as this conversation might be, I feel that you are trying to distract me or maybe give me a migraine.”

“Is it working?” Tessa smiled. “I have drugs in my bathroom that will fix you right up.”

“I didn’t hear that.” The officer didn’t sound amused. “I know you’re kidding. Right?”

All three of them spoke in unison. “Right.”

“Agent Martin, are you off the books? I mean, seems to me if you weren’t, you’d have called your supervisor by now who in turn would have my boss up my…” He stole a look at Tessa. “Well, he'd be pulling rank."

"Officer Michaels, I don't care what Chase says about you. Your manners are impeccable." Tessa reached out and patted him on the shoulder. "Would you like a cup of coffee?"

"I thought you didn't have any coffee," Agent Martin reminded her.

"My bad. Guess I had a brain freeze caused by the worry over your injuries."

Agent Martin sighed. "I see your propensity for lying has not changed."

"She's got homemade sugar cookies, too." Chase reached out his hand to pull the agent to his feet.

"Tessa, I hope you know Captain Hunter is attracted to you because of your culinary prowess. I know it's hard to hear, but I always considered you a friend, so I feel it necessary to tell you." He stood erect and pulled back his shoulders and moved toward the kitchen when she slipped her arm through his.

"I've missed you, Dennis."

"Humph," was his only response as he let her lead him to the kitchen. She turned back to the other two. "Well come on," she ordered.

She heard Chase's comment to the officer. "The woman is a master at calming the beast. Better be on your guard."

"Don't I know it. Guess it doesn't have the same effect on Pastor Paxton's wife. She was fit to be tied. Blamed Tessa for everything. Also accused her of knocking her down in the snow. Any truth to that?"

"I can neither confirm nor deny that allegation."

"You sound like one of those government jerks."

"Again, I can neither—"

Tessa rushed back to the two men and huffed as she grabbed their hands and tugged them toward the kitchen. "Yes! I confess! I pushed the bit—I mean the woman down in the snow. Actually, I tripped her. I really did try to help her up, but she slipped right out of my hand."

"Told you. She's a liar. If you look up the word 'humbug' in the dictionary, Tessa's picture is there." Agent Martin spoke as he tried to keep cookie crumbs from tumbling out of his mouth.

"What's a dictionary?" Officer Michaels joked. "How old are

you?"

Tessa smiled at the disgruntled agent and poured him a fresh cup of coffee. "I think I hear the patter of little feet upstairs. Better go settle down the troops."

"Want me to go, too?" Chase asked as she strolled by him and patted his abdomen.

Agent Martin snarled. "You're going to make me hurl, Hunter."

Tessa stopped and smiled up at the man who had made such a difference in her life. "I got this. Why don't you start the interrogation of Agent Martin while I'm gone? You're scarier than me."

"That's up for debate." The agent grabbed another cookie.

Tessa lowered her voice and, with the best Austrian accent she could muster, spoke the words from everyone's favorite Terminator. "I'll be back."

Chapter 6

"Mom, what is going on?" Sean Patrick slipped out of his room to question Tessa. "Is everything okay?"

Tessa came to sit on the edge of his twin bed. Daniel, now asleep, had an arm hanging off the side of the bed. Heather had been drowsy and roused enough to receive her hug and kiss good night. But Sean Patrick's curiosity, apparently, had not been satisfied enough to succumb to a silly thing like sleep. She moved his lock of dark hair back from his forehead.

"Yes. Everything is fine. Do you remember FBI Agent Martin who helped Daddy?"

He started to nod then threw up his hands in doubt as she gently pushed him down onto his pillow.

"Turns out, he had a fender bender and bumped his head. Lost his phone in the snow and thought he'd try and find us." She smiled. "He was a mess by the time he got here. Poor guy. I expect him to leave soon. I'm not sure he should be alone, however."

"Why was he in town?"

Leave it to Sean Patrick to begin his own interrogation.

"Business, I guess. You know those guys don't talk about what they do or an ongoing case. Our friend, Officer Michaels, is still—visiting with him."

"I bet Chase will get to the bottom of it."

"Do you like Chase?" It seemed to be the perfect time to ask.

"Most of the time. Is he…like…your boyfriend?"

"Why do you ask?"

"Isn't Dad coming back home?" His voice was edged with a mixture of sadness and uneasiness.

"Sean Patrick, I know this is really hard to understand, but Daddy has a new life now. I miss him, too, but fortunately we've remained friends and both love you guys very much."

"Didn't he want us anymore?"

"Of course, he did! He does!" she insisted. "I also explained about our marriage being unlawful. Right?"

"Why couldn't Dad just fix it? He's a lawyer."

"Some things can't be fixed, Sean Patrick. My life is with you kids. I'm thinking of moving back to Tennessee, near Mimi and Pops. Would you like that?"

"What about Dad? Would he come, too?"

"I don't know, sweetheart." She kissed him on the forehead. "But know this—he will always love you, no matter what."

"Chase acts like he wants to be our dad."

"He's never had a family, and he's impressed with us." She chuckled. "And I'm impressed with him. He makes me happy."

Sean Patrick pulled his mother down and hugged her. "Dad wasn't always nice to you, was he?"

"Well let's just say, he didn't always make me happy." She stood and tucked the covers around him. "I'll get any twisted and diabolical information from Officer Michaels and Agent Martin to share with you. Now, go to sleep. You've got a full workday tomorrow."

"Yes, ma'am."

Tessa eased down the stairs, picking up a sock, a doll dress and, what resembled a walkie-talkie. There was a basket on the library table at the bottom of the steps. When she set such things there, they needed a forever home in twenty-four hours or the trash would adopt them with extreme prejudice. No takebacks—well, except for the socks. If they didn't find the mate, then the abandoned and forgotten socks would be paired with one of her choice. The culprit the original belonged would then have to wear the creative duo for one whole day. She rarely had to do this anymore.

Male voices, serious with a hint of bewilderment, drifted quietly from the kitchen. She hoped this wasn't going to mess with her Christmas plans. She wanted the Hallmark movie version, not the Die-Hard version. The last couple of years had messed with her sense of humor, faith, joy, and optimistic attitude. Then Captain Hunter showed up, like he always did in a rough patch, and confessed his love for her. After that clap of thunder, everything began to fall into place, in spite of a few hiccups.

For the first time in her adult life, her heart grew content. There were still days when it was hard to trust a man, believe the world wasn't about to self-destruct, or that this life the captain was trying to give her would work out. She still longed to see the life around her through Heather's eyes. Every day, she had long talks with her daughter to touch that goodness and magical spirit she, herself, once held. The boys, although rambunctious, nearly always made her laugh, giving her a sense of pride in their toughness. In spite of their father not being present most of the time, she had taught them how to play baseball, throw a football, and basic karate. Even Heather could spiral a football better than most boys in the neighborhood twice her age.

Together, the four of them barely noticed Robert was no longer there on a daily basis. Their lives had not changed that much. Fortunately, Chase showed up and took over the duties Robert should have been doing, like mowing the grass, playing catch with the boys, and listening to Heather's nonsensible angst concerning rainbow unicorns and why they couldn't live with the tree fairies any longer. This was all while sipping water tea with his pinky held out and a fluffy boa around his neck.

Heather had sanded a great number of rough edges from the mighty Captain Chase Hunter. He adored the child, and the feeling appeared to be mutual. Sometimes, she forgot and called him Dad. Whether he corrected her or she realized the mistake, it didn't appear to bother either of them. If anything, he would send her a sly look with a crooked grin and whisper to Tessa it was time to make their relationship known and tie up the loose ends.

"You're waiting for things to be perfect," Chase reminded her one night when they were alone in her Sacramento apartment. "There's never going to be a perfect time. You're afraid, and I get that. So am I. We've both been through hell and back. I'm not going to let you down, Tessa. I'm not Robert and"—this is usually where things got uncomfortable—"I'm not Darya."

Roman Darya Petrov was a half-Kyrgyz, half-Russian tribesman who'd kidnapped her, forced her into a marriage, and filled her head with all kinds of promises he couldn't keep. But she'd fallen in love with him, nonetheless. That relationship had come to an explosive end, and Chase was left to pick up the pieces he wasn't sure would ever fit back together.

The truth of their three-way relationship still got in the way at times, but the fact was, she loved only Chase. Listening to his deep voice in her kitchen convinced her that this Christmas would be the magical one to bring completeness to her life.

"What are you boys talking about? Anything I should know?" Tessa eased up onto one of the barstools and grabbed a sugar cookie. "Did you guys eat all of these? This is the last one."

"Agent shoved a few in his pockets," Chase grumbled flippantly. "He's a bit uncouth, if you'll remember."

"I never believed that, Dennis," she said playfully as she waved her napkin at him.

"Good. I never believed all those things he said about you, either." The agent spoke sarcastically, as Tessa leveled a stern look at Chase.

Chase threw up his hands and shook a fist at the agent before addressing his wife. "You can't trust anything the FBI says, Tessa. You know that. The only thing I ever said about you was that you had a great imagination."

"That's code for liar," the agent voiced matter-of-factly. "I know it hurts, but I feel it's my duty to tell you after all we've been through."

Tessa jabbed the now-laughing Officer Michaels. "All right, you guys," she said. "Enough. Mr. Special Agent Martin, why are you really here?"

Chase came to stand next to Tessa and slipped a hand across her back before the agent sobered. "It seems that Heather's little friend Kelly might be in danger."

A wave of panic filled Tessa. "What does that mean?"

"It means," Officer Michaels offered, "that the Nativity fire may have been a distraction to grab Kelly and run. I don't think he started it, but he was there checking things out."

"But why? Is there a kidnapping ring in the area? Oh my gosh. Oh my gosh," Tessa fretted.

Chase rubbed her shoulder. "Not exactly."

Agent Martin sipped his coffee before speaking. "Did you know Kelly was adopted?"

"Now that you mention it, I do remember hearing something about that. The Parkers had waited years to adopt. Mrs. Parker worked at St. Clarice Hospital in Seattle as a social worker. The mother wanted to give her up for adoption. The Parkers signed on as foster parents until they could make it legal." Tessa patted her heart. "They are such wonderful parents."

"Yeah, well what you don't know is that after two years, they packed up and ran with Kelly. That adoption is still pending but expected to be completed in a few weeks, maybe sooner. Although the birth mother died in a car accident, someone else, we think the father, materialized and wants the child."

Chase sighed and shook his head. "It gets worse. The father has ties with organized crime, Tessa."

Agent Martin wiped his mouth and fingered a few crumbs from the plate. He quickly told them about the last six weeks, trying to find him after he escaped custody. "I've been so close at catching him. It's not been on the news because he has connections with a Mexican cartel. He's a big-time thief and has been connected to several murders, although that couldn't be proven. However, his girlfriend, Kelly's birth mother, had plenty of evidence to share. She was slotted to go into the witness protection program when she died."

"You were hurt and came here. Was there more to that?" Officer Michaels inquired.

"I'm afraid he thinks Heather is his daughter, not Kelly. He saw them together tonight and probably several other times. That's why I wanted to get here, since I chased him this far. He ran me off the road." He shot Officer Michaels a narrowed look. "And I did contact headquarters in Sacramento. Expect to be under my thumb for a few days. Your boss will see to it."

"What can we do?" Chase asked.

"Stay out of the way," Agent Martin growled. "The Parkers, oh, not their real name, have been in the witness protection program all this time. The birth mother did a video confession as to the father's criminal activities and even kept some pretty damning books for evidence. That was the real reason she didn't keep the baby. She was afraid of what would become of her child. No one knew about Kelly. As I said earlier, the father, Gallo, escaped a prison back East. He's a bad one."

"How did he find out they were here?" Tessa poured the agent more coffee.

"The Parkers, I'm guessing, used the evidence after the birth mother died, to get him convicted?" Officer Michaels speculated.

"Bingo," the agent snapped and leveled his finger at him like a gun.

"And now he's looking for payback and his daughter." Tessa realized her children were in more danger than first believed.

"I mentioned to the pastor, after it came over the wire, that a possible escaped convict was headed to this part of California." Officer Michaels propped his elbows on the island. "I mentioned it to any church or organization with outdoor activities. Pretty easy for someone to blend in since a lot of people come to Grass Valley during the Christmas parades, craft fairs, and children's programs. Anyone up to mischief could take advantage of the good in people. I had no idea the Parkers were in the witness protection program, so that ups my concern."

"Oh dear. I sure hope Ellen Paxton is careful during all of this," Tessa said coyly.

"Maybe you should just arrest Tessa now, and that will be one less person we have to worry about breaking the law," Agent Martin quipped.

In spite of the seriousness of the matter, the group released a good-natured chuckle.

Chapter 7

Chase poured himself a cup of coffee. For once, he'd stayed at Tessa's house instead of the Ervins next door. They had been his substitute family for several years. Agent Martin was in no shape to drive and took Tessa up on her offer to sleep on her family room couch. Officer Michaels had been called out on another matter and didn't return.

"I'll sleep on the living room couch," Chase declared as he grabbed the red blanket covered in snowflakes. Tessa's disarming smile made him groan. "This has got to end, Tessa. I don't like sleeping alone."

"We could get a cat."

"Or we could just make it official."

Their kisses lingered until Tessa gently pushed him out of her embrace. "I want that, too. We'll talk to the kids."

"When?"

"Let's get through this thing with little Kelly and the Parkers first. Then I'm all yours."

He grinned. "You've been all mine pretty consistently." He chuckled softly, causing her to step toward him and shush him, while looking toward the staircase. Wrapping his arms around her, he once more knew he'd struck gold the day she came into his life.

"Okay. I'm talking to Robert, too."

"I'll do that."

"You will not. At least, not without me."

"Can we talk about this later?" She kissed him briefly on the lips and stepped far enough away he couldn't steal her back. "He still thinks I'm going to return to him and ask for forgiveness."

"And I'm still thinking I should have dropped him off the Bay Bridge when I had a chance."

"Shh. You don't mean that."

He nodded slowly. "I pretty much do."

In spite of the couch being more comfortable than expected, his legs were too long and his body too wide for such furniture. After several hours, he made a pallet on the floor and slept for what was left of the night. He didn't totally feel relaxed knowing someone was looking for Kelly and might mistake Heather for her little friend. Having spent many nights as a soldier, being alert even when asleep, he felt right at home.

He heard the shower turn on upstairs in the master bathroom about the same time the children stirred. No sneaking up there now without getting the third degree from the kids. While he held the coffee to his lips, he let the previous night's events run through his brain. Had he seen anything suspicious? Was someone out of place? The boys were absolutely guilty in causing the fire to start. Maybe because he intervened when he had, Kelly's birth father hadn't taken a chance in coming forward.

"Morning." It was Agent Martin. He yawned and scratched his head before inhaling deeply. "Got more coffee?"

Chase tilted his head toward the coffeepot on the counter. "Help yourself."

"Are you cooking breakfast?" He glanced around the open-concept kitchen that joined the family room where he'd spent the night. "You seem to be Mr. Domestication now."

"Screw you," Chase offered. "I know you meant that as an insult."

Agent Martin grinned and joined him at the island to drink his coffee. "Just can't imagine you and Tessa playing house is all." He chuckled then pretended to draw a circle on his chest. "She needs one of those skull and crossbones on her clothes to alert anyone who comes close."

"I heard that." Tessa padded into the kitchen barefoot. "I wouldn't need a warning sign if you misfits hadn't dragged me into your lair of half-truths, blah, blah, blah."

"She always this cranky in the morning?" the agent asked offhandedly.

"I can neither confirm nor deny such a statement," Chase answered straight-faced.

"Aww. Thank you, Chase." Tessa accepted the cup of coffee he poured her.

"I'm going to run upstairs and take a shower. I'll take Sean Patrick to church and make sure nothing is amiss there," Chase said.

"Thanks. Dennis, do you need a ride some place?" Tessa opened the refrigerator door. "How about some eggs?"

"Aw, this is the reason Chase is turning into a softy. You fill him with sugar cookies at night then cook high-protein food to keep his constitution off-balance, all the while you're sweet-talking him." The agent poured himself another cup of coffee. "Anyway, I need a ride to check on my car. Don't want to go to Sacramento with things happening here. I might need to swing by to get a rental if the car can't be fixed."

"I'm going to be late as it is. Tessa?" Chase walked backward toward the stairs then stole a look up.

"Sure. I would love to—handle Dennis. No problem at all." Her smile carried a hint of mischief. "We're overdue for a chat, Dennis."

Agent Martin frowned and rolled his eyes. "I'll take those eggs now. And you can't sweet-talk me into anything, so get over yourself. All those half-baked friends of yours at Enigma might fall for your angelic ruse, but I'm on to you. You're as bad as they come."

Light laughter escaped from Chase as he headed up the steps. Agent Martin might pretend he didn't like Tessa, but he still had gone to bat for her several times. He'd even pulled her ex-husband out of a jam that could have sent him to prison, along with losing his license to practice law. With his help, the guy came out smelling like a rose. Or, maybe it was because he owed Enigma. Either way, he thought the agent enjoyed baiting Tessa and pretending she was a nuisance. Apparently, she saw right through his nonsense.

"You're still here?" Sean Patrick came out of his room and stopped as Chase was about to enter his mom's bedroom. "Spend the night?"

"On the living room couch," he answered flatly. Why should a kid make him feel nervous? He'd stood up to the Taliban, fought Syrian terrorists as well as drug dealers and dictators of third world countries, yet this kid, arching an eyebrow at him as he slowly crossed his arms across his chest made him uneasy. "Agent Martin couldn't drive home, of course, so I kept an eye on him to make sure he was okay during the night. He got the family room."

"Where's my mom?"

"Fixing Agent Martin breakfast. If you hurry, you can interrogate him and show him how it's done."

The kid smirked.

For some unearthly reason, Chase felt the overpowering need to explain why he was standing at his mother's bedroom door. "Going to get a quick shower. I'll be down in a minute."

"Oh. Well, if you need any underwear, my dad still has a few pair in the bottom dresser drawer—you know—for when he spends the night and needs a shower." He grinned then barreled down the stairs.

Chase stood frozen for a few seconds and decided this kind of intimidation had to end.

CHAPTER 8

Anthony Gallo hated the snow. Miami didn't have snow, and having to be here for Christmas rather than under a palm tree, sipping his favorite drink while he watched a parade of girls in string bikinis, annoyed him. The air smelled different up here in the Sierras. That also annoyed him since he preferred the smell of salt water and the sounds of seabirds dipping in the waves. But, at least, it wasn't prison.

The transfer had been routine, except it wasn't. A freak accident had enabled him to escape in a highly wooded area in North Carolina. It took several weeks to make his way to Seattle where he'd discovered his girlfriend had lived, only to discover she'd died years earlier. The big news was he had a child. A daughter. Through a few of his contacts, he'd learned she'd been adopted, before the trail went cold, just like this miserable place called Grass Valley, California.

In his line of work, a number of people were beholden to him, so he didn't have to draw attention to himself by snooping around to find information. No need to threaten or intimidate. There were others who did that for him. He would grab his daughter and escape to Mexico where he already had a cartel waiting for him to take control of part of the drug business.

Crushing a cigarette beneath his foot caused slushy snow to spill into his shoe. When he kicked it off, a man approached, taking in the nearby businesses and occasionally pausing at several shop windows, as if interested in the merchandise. Although morning, the Christmas lights still twinkled, with a few shopkeepers coming outside to salt the icy sidewalk for soon-to-be customers.

"You're out early." Anthony Gallo took in the shorter man from head to toe. "I want an update."

"The church has a workday today. The fire was put out pretty fast. I thought we agreed you wouldn't be there last night."

"I don't answer to you. I'll do what I want," he growled. "I want my kid, so I had a look around."

"There will be church volunteers today and some people I think from the park service. It joins the church grounds. Good will goes a long way here. Mostly cleanup." He handed him a plastic bag. "This has the park logo on it if you decide to be useful."

"Sure, why not?"

"The police are looking for you."

"How do they know I'm here?"

"Overheard the pastor talking to one of the local police officers the other day. I'm sure by now he's passed it along to one of our security guys. Military. Army, I think."

"Army guy? What's he doing in a place like this? Doesn't he have a war someplace he should be dealing with?"

"How do I know? He's carrying a gun on his hip and looks like he chews barbed wire for breakfast. Tried to talk to him last night before the fire. Several of us wanted to get to know him since he's dating one of the young moms." He smiled. "She's a looker, too. Hear she has a few sketchy friends. The church ladies say she has a taste for roughness."

"You pay attention to what I told you to do. She the adopted mom to my daughter?"

"Nah. She's dating G.I. Joe. He interrupted the unexpected distraction last night. I really don't know much about anyone there because I haven't attended regularly for a couple of years. Started back a several months ago after we talked. Besides, I thought it would be good for business this close to Christmas."

"How Christian of you," Anthony snipped.

"We're square now, right?"

"We're square when I get my kid."

"I want nothing to do with that. I could go to jail. I don't want to go back."

"You'll do as I say until I take her. And if I want you to do more, then you'll do it."

"We had a deal," he protested.

Anthony frowned as he turned his head to see if anyone was watching before he grabbed the man by the front of his coat, tightened his grip, and pulled him into the space between two buildings. The man instinctively pulled at Anthony's hands until he freed himself.

"The deal has been amended. I didn't know this place was crawling with It's a Wonderful Life characters or that there would be a muscle-headed soldier watching the place like he was walking the streets of Afghanistan."

"And if I say no?" The man stepped back and smoothed the front of his coat.

"Guess I'll put you on the Grass Valley P.D.'s radar. I'm sure they'd love to know we used to be cellmates and that thanks to you, that little accident that helped me escape was your doing."

"I did no such thing."

"By the time they realize that, I'll be long gone with my daughter, sipping tequila on a beach in Cozumel."

"Some father you'll be."

This caused Anthony to laugh. "How would you know? Just do what you're told. Now here is what I'm thinking." He lowered his voice, causing the man to bow his head to carefully.

~~~~

Chase enjoyed the feel of a hammer in his hands. When he was a kid, he'd tinkered with tools to help his father repair their simple home and clinic in rural China. His parents were medical missionaries and treated the sick and injured the best they could with what few supplies they could purchase. The sponsors back in the States sent them money each month and although with that amount, anyone could live like a king in a communist country, they used most of it for their practice. Although not officially
~~~~

connected with a church, Chase remembered how they demonstrated their faith through serving.

As a kid, he'd often had to help out at the clinic doing various chores. One of those was repairs. Now, here he was, making repairs on a church structure, something he'd promised he'd never do again. He'd grown to hate that life, what it had done to his family, and how he'd watched the government turn on them. With his sister, he'd escaped in the middle of the night after seeing their parents dragged from their home. To this day, he could still hear them begging then praying for the soldiers just before rapid-fire gunshots exploded the darkness, followed by silence.

Thanks to Buddhist monks who had received medical care from his parents, and shared what little they had, Chase and his sister were taken over the mountains into Tibet to find freedom.

"What are you thinking about?" Sean Patrick's voice broke his backward reflection.

"That it feels good to be working with my hands again." Chase eyed him, and once more the kid reminded him of his own cocky attitude that got him into a lot of trouble. "Used to do this kind of work when I lived in China."

"Yeah? Cool."

For a second, Chase raised his chin in suspicion, wondering if the kid wasn't planning to circumvent him with a distraction. "That's me. Mr. Cool."

Sean Patrick smirked. "I wouldn't go that far."

"Why aren't you working?"

"Taking a break. Pastor's orders."

"Didn't see his boy."

"Said he had a sore throat from inhaling the smoke last night. His mom wanted him to stay home."

Chase could feel his eyebrow arch and his jaw tighten and release. "Do you believe him?"

"Do you?"

"No."

"So, what are we gonna do about it, big guy?"

He noticed the kid took the identical stance as he took and tilted his head much the same way as he scanned the area with narrowed eyes. Part of him wanted to laugh, but the rest of him felt proud.

"I'll think of something. Come with me and I'll help you knock this out so we can blow this Popsicle stand." He raised his free hand for a high five, and Sean Patrick was quick to slap his hand.

He took a deep breath and moved toward where he'd been assigned. "Let's do this, Captain."

There was no doubt the kid was destined for military life. He already wore the attitude as if it were a badge of honor. Whether his mother knew it or not, he'd talked to Chase once about attending West Point. Since Chase had gotten his first degree there, Sean Patrick felt he could reassure his mother when the time came to "pull the trigger," as he called it. What the kid hadn't expected was hearing how difficult it was to get in and what was required once you made it.

"Mom knows the president so why wouldn't I get in?"

As the boy stepped away, Chase reached out and pulled him back. "Sean Patrick, that stunt last night could have been a black mark against you if the cops had chosen to make it an issue. Keep your nose clean and don't be a hothead if you want into West Point."

"It was my sister and her friend."

"I hear ya. Next time, don't get caught, numbskull. I can teach you a few tricks. That bully isn't done with you. I know you're going to call him a lying momma's boy next time you see him. Let someone else do that. Be the hero. Those little girls are going to get the word out and, by that time, all you'll need is a red cape to look like Superman."

Sean Patrick grinned and took the stance of the famous superhero as if he'd been practicing his whole life. "I don't care what Heather and Daniel say; I think you're an okay guy."

"Gee, Sean Patrick. You don't know how relieved I am to hear it."

"No problem." He fist-bumped his arm. "Keep up the good work."

Chase shook his head as he followed the boy to his work station. Heaven help him, but he really did like the kid in spite of his knee-jerk decision-making skills and devious manipulation techniques. It was like looking in a mirror.

CHAPTER 9

Before heading out for the day, Tessa watched Agent Martin wolf down his second stack of pancakes and wondered how long it'd been since he'd eaten a homecooked meal. She became aware there was little she knew about him other than he'd been divorced several times. Did he have any living family members? Was the FBI his only attachment to other people? The way he kept hanging on to each word coming out of the kids' mouths, she wondered if he was interested or trying to gather more information to put in her file labeled Don't Believe A Word She Says.

He glanced over at her sipping her third cup of coffee and locked stares with her as he pushed his plate away. "Do your kids always talk so much?" he asked as Daniel and Heather scooted off their stools and ran into the family room.

"Aren't they precious?" She smiled after them.

"How would I know? I've never been around kids. From what Chase has told me, they're a lot like the Taliban."

Tessa bristled but decided to relax, figuring the agent was trying to rile her up against Chase. "I never thought of that." Her mock surprise was almost convincing.

"No wonder he fits right in with this tribe. So, you two are an official couple or what?"

"Agent Martin, are you asking as a friend or as a nosey FBI Agent? If it's the latter, then it isn't any of your business. And why on earth would you seek me out last night other than to tell me about the kidnapping possibility?"

"Isn't that enough?" he growled.

"I think you were coming to check on us. To make sure we were okay."

"You are so full of yourself, Tessa. Everyone thinks you're the sweetheart of Enigma, but I know better. Remember, I saw firsthand when you teamed up with that Irish assassin trash not so long ago during another Christmas."

"What is your point, Agent Martin? I mean, Dennis."

"You stole from the highway department, probably an accessory to attempted murder, evaded law enforcement, and assaulted a federal agent. That would be me." He reached for the coffeepot. "Mind if I have the last cup?"

She retrieved the pot and poured him the last of the dark brew. "I can make another pot."

"No. Thank you, though. And don't think feeding me, letting me sleep on your couch, and talking all soft and comforting to me will change my mind on how I feel about you."

Tessa chuckled and replaced the coffeepot on the stand. "Okay, Scrooge, thanks for being honest. Finish your coffee, and I'll take you to see if your car is drivable or if you need a rental. Heather is going to the Ervins to make Christmas cookies for treats for the cookie exchange at church."

"Those your neighbors? The ones Chase pretends to stay with when he actually slips over here after the kids go to bed? You know they're cut from the same cloth as your Irish assassin friend, right?"

Tessa shifted her weight to one hip as she glared at the agent. "I've had just about enough of your negativity and insults. I'm sort of glad now I added a little something to your last cup of coffee."

A look of horror crossed his face. "You didn't."

"Guess we'll find out by tomorrow if you have to call poison control." She deepened her voice and spoke slowly.

"You're a funny lady."

"So. I'm. Told." She patted his shoulder and took his cup. "Just kidding. I'll take Heather next door. You be ready to go when

I get back. Oh, and I have a little favor to ask of you on the way."

"The answer is no, whatever it is."

"Still feeling okay, Agent Martin?" She cackled like a witch.

The agent lowered his head to hide a smile as she walked past him. Now who was the softy?

~~~~

Chase walked with Pastor Paxton around the repaired Nativity structure, with Deacon Monroe and the pudgy insurance man, Horace, he thought. There was a great deal of hand gestures, head bobbing, and a few "thank you, Jesus" comments. He was keenly aware the pastor took two steps to his one and rubbed his chin from time to time as if he were trying to think of something important to say. The man wasn't much taller than Tessa, and she probably outweighed him by ten pounds.

The pastor wasn't a bad speaker on Sunday mornings. The reason Chase knew this was because at first, he'd listened a few times to him online. Reconnaissance was part of who he was, or at least that was what he told Tessa so she'd stop bugging him to go with them on Sunday. He reflected back on how he tried to outmaneuver her with zero success.

"I'm not going, so I'm basically saving your life," he confessed as she narrowed her eyes. "I'm pretty sure lightning would strike me and you might be burned in the process." He kissed her on the temple. "You're welcome."

"I want us to set a good example for the kids. They should know there are things bigger than themselves. We're a family."

"Actually, we aren't. Not yet. I'm not sure why you're stalling on telling the kids and Robert about us. Am I auditioning for head of the tribe or what?" he growled, getting irritated.

The discussion got him the silent treatment for a couple of days. He knew she was scared. Scared of making a wrong decision. Trusting one more man who would either cheat and lie like the kids' father or be another Roman Darya Petrov, who took her love and almost destroyed her. He decided not to back down and remain steady until she got over being pissed at him.

In the end, he occasionally went with her to church, and she promised to make their relationship official.
~~~~

"I love you, Captain Hunter," she confessed as she pulled him into her bed a few nights after the confrontation. The kids were with their father, so make-up sex was even better when he wasn't at fault. "I can always depend on you."

"Always," he said, taking her like there was no tomorrow because, in their line of work, that could happen.

But, for now, here he stood, in charge of rebuilding a Nativity structure because his stepson had taken it upon himself to protect his little sister and her friend. There were worse ways to spend a Saturday morning. Sean Patrick stuck right with him and, with those long legs of his, he kept up better than the pastor. The boy showed several improvements but was ignored. Chase elbowed him and then gave a thumbs-up.

"Proud of you, boy. You done good."

"Thanks, Captain. We make a good team. Daniel and I were talking, and maybe we could buy a Christmas tree to plant outside the lean-to. It needs something. Douglas Tree Farm has a few outside Albertson's Grocery Store. You know, a way to give back, and all that."

Chase couldn't help but notice how the kid cut his narrowed gaze over at the pastor and smirked. He figured the embarrassment creeping up into Paxton's face, the color of a candy cane, was punishment enough for not insisting his son participate.

"Sean Patrick, collect the tools and make sure they are returned to each worker who brought them. Let's get that tree and hurry back to plant it before the weather turns bad."

"But…" he moaned. Chase cocked his head slightly to stare solemn faced at the boy. "Yes, sir."

Chase watched him stomp through the snow then called out to him. "Get Daniel to help you."

"What else do you need, Pastor?" Chase pulled his hoodie up since the wind had risen and took a deep breath. A stream of fog materialized as he exhaled.

"I appreciate your help." The pastor lifted a hand at the other two men. "You guys, too. I need to go around and thank the others before they leave. See you all tonight? Chili, hot dogs, and cookie exchange. Fundraiser for our food pantry, too. Donations of any kind welcome."

"You've been beating us over the head with that information

for a month." Deacon grinned.

"So, I have," Paxton chuckled.

It didn't take long to find the tree lot and choose a five-foot pine. Planting the tree was a group effort. Deacon Monroe had already dug the hole by the time they returned. There was a great deal of grunting and flippant remarks from the boys, but they got the job done without much help from him.

Chase's phone vibrated. Turning away from the boys, he noticed a man watching them from near the prayer garden. He didn't recognize him from the night before, and it was his habit to check and memorize his surroundings. The man wore a sock hat low over his brow. With a quick pivot, the stranger continued shoveling snow along the walk where visitors had stomped an icy coating off their boots.

"Chase," he said into his phone while continuing to watch the new guy.

"Are you close to getting finished?" It was Tessa.

"Just done. What's up?"

"I'm stuck at the garage with our favorite FBI agent who is trying to bully them into fixing his car first."

"Maybe you should take over and bat those baby blues to speed things up."

"I may have to. Anyway, the Ervins took Heather to dance rehearsal, and someone has to be there to pick her up."

"No problem. Text me the address. Sean Patrick and Daniel say they have hockey practice, so I'll drop them off."

"Perfect. Daniel needs to be there ASAP."

After hanging up, Chase noticed the stranger had disappeared. He did a quick search but found no one. He quizzed his two new friends who had taken to being his devoted shadow. Turned out, after asking one of the workers, figured it was probably the new custodian and harmless, not to worry. If he didn't leave now, the boys would be late for practice. After dropping them at hockey practice, he headed to the theater where Heather was practicing for her dance recital.

Upon entering, he saw her sitting on the steps that led down to the stage. Kelly was next to her with a chubby arm around her shoulders. Chase heard tiny sobs and saw her shoulders bob up and down. He scanned the area, wondering why the girls weren't being supervised.

Squatting down next to her, he waited for her to notice he was close. When she turned her little face toward him, wet tears running down to soak her pink lips, his heart lurched. Taking both his thumbs, he wiped away the tears then pushed a wayward curl out of her eyes. How many times had he done that to her mother?

"Baby Cakes," —which was what he always called her— "who should I thump for making my best girl cry?" She smiled, giving him permission to scoot into position next to her.

"It's okay, Heather," Kelly consoled, rubbing her friend on the back.

Heather stuck her lip out and shook her head as she stood and looked longingly at the captain. "Nothin'."

He gathered her in his arms, and she nuzzled her face in his neck.

Would being a dad always be like this? One minute, you were putting out fires, next minute, your heart was breaking because someone messed with your kid? Maybe he should have stayed with fighting the Taliban. No emotional consequences from those guys or on his part as well.

"What's up, Miss Kelly?" he asked as he reached out to pat her knee.

She sighed. "Her daddy didn't come to rehearsal, and if he doesn't, then she can't do the daddy-daughter dance at the recital."

Chase began to fake a cry, sniffing and wiping at his eyes as Heather jerked back and put her little hands on his cheek. "Chasey, why are you crying?"

"I thought you were going to ask me to do the daddy-daughter dance." He bowed his head and covered his face with his large hands.

Kelly jumped up and clapped her hands. "I know. Have the captain be your daddy. I think he might be smart enough to learn it."

Chase raised his eyes to see the light come back to Heather's eyes. "Please let me try, Heather. I'll work hard."

She put her hands on her hips. "Well, will you show up and dance with me in front of millions of people who are coming to the recital?"

"Millions?" He wasn't sure there were that many people in this part of California.

"Millions. Maybe more. Like thousands," she insisted.

"I'm your guy. Let's do this!" He stood and towered over his new boss.

"You're big," Kelly said in amazement.

Heather grabbed his hand and pulled him down the steps. "Yes, but he's such a teddy bear."

"Heather, I've warned you not to say that in public."

"Sorry. He's such a badass."

"Well, we're going to have to come to a kind of understanding on your choice of pet names for me."

"Whatever. Let's go."

CHAPTER 10

Tessa was glad to be dropping Dennis Martin off at the shop. Although the shop was overwhelmed with jobs, they did a quick once-over for an FBI agent. After he explained he needed the vehicle to search for an escaped felon, they were full of Christmas gratitude. She waited in the car and caught up on emails, text messages, and a video sent by Chase as to the progress of the new Nativity arrangement. This one even had a Christmas tree.

"As you can see," Chase began as he aimed the camera toward Sean Patrick and Daniel who were stringing lights on the tree outside the crude structure, "we now have a Christmas tree, thanks to the boys. They took their own money to buy it. We even planted it."

"Those are expensive this year."

"Well, since it was for the church Nativity after the fiasco last night, the tree lot cut the price in half. They were pretty amused."

"Half off could still be a little pricey for them."

"I might have chipped in a little, but they promised to pay me back their share when they got home."

"Aww. You're the best," she cooed.

"We both know that isn't true."

"I'm not talking about Christmas trees, Chase."

He turned the camera toward his face. "Seriously, Tessa? I'm at a church."

"Gotta go. Here comes Scrooge FBI Martin." Tessa clicked off and powered down the window as Dennis leaned down to talk. "What's the verdict?"

"Not much to worry about. Won't be pretty for a while. They bent the bumper back in place enough to drive then installed a new windshield. Suggested I get some new tires, although that wasn't caused by the accident. Planned to do that anyway, after Christmas."

"I know a guy who can make you a good deal, Dennis."

"Let me guess. He's one of your underworld sketchy friends who will shave a few bucks off if you bake him some cookies."

"What do you have against my cookies? People love my cookies."

"Men love your cookies. Women hate you, and it's not because of your cookies—or maybe it is, only it's not really cookies."

"Don't be vulgar," she retorted. "Do you want my contact or not?"

"As long as he doesn't have a record or his picture isn't in the post office, I'm in."

"I can't promise either of those things."

"Then you'd better make me some cookies to sweeten the deal with him."

"Done. Now what?"

"You can go on about your business. I'll drive out of here within the hour. Got some work to do, and I'll get a room someplace."

"Oh, I hate for you to do that. You're welcome to use the couch again."

"No thanks. I think that Barbie doll I found between the cushions last night goosed me. I want none of her stuff another night."

"No wonder you're single, Dennis." She began to power up the window, knowing Dennis had leaned in a little too far. He tried to step back but it was too late; his tie was caught. She arched an eyebrow and leveled a devilish smirk at him then started the car.

"Very funny, Tessa. Roll down the damn window," he

ordered.

Tessa reached into the console and withdrew a pair of scissors she kept on hand for emergencies. Before he could protest, Tessa had snipped off his tie.

Dennis jerked back and yelled some unflattering comments. Tessa pushed her face against the glass and crossed her eyes. He quickly took out his phone and snapped a picture.

"I'm sending that in my Christmas cards to all your Enigma psychos." He shook his phone at her as she drove off laughing but managed to blow him a kiss.

~~~~

Chase pulled in the driveway that circled in front of the Victorian country house Tessa called home. It was far different than the other houses in the California-chic neighborhood. He guessed it had a lot to do with her upbringing in rural Tennessee. There were times he'd stop and stare at it, remembering his times spent in the mountains of North Carolina with his grandfather.

Tessa had expressed interest in moving back to east Tennessee, maybe to Gatlinburg, just outside of the Smokey Mountain National Park. It would be just a short drive to the Qualla Reservation where his grandfather still lived. He wasn't sure when he'd taken to having daydreams about the future. Probably had something to do with the blue-eyed beauty he married or the unicorn princess singing "Away in a Manger" in the back seat.

"Are we getting out, Chasey?" she asked mid-song, which snapped him back to the here and now.

"Sure. Just admiring all your mom's Christmas decorations." He unbuckled his seat belt and opened the door. When he walked around to help Heather, she had already relieved herself of the constraints holding her in place. She giggled and fell into his arms when he reached in to lift her out then added a hug around his neck.

"I helped."

"I remember. So did I." He set her feet on the shoveled driveway.

"Daddy never would help. Said all the fuss was ridiculous. But
~~~~

he liked it once we were done."

"I'll bet," he grumbled.

"He did offer to come help this year, but Mommy said you had already pitched in and done it."

"I didn't know that. I'll bet he was disappointed." He held her hand as she jumped to each step and counted.

"Maybe. Sean Patrick said he was pissed."

"I need to speak to Sean Patrick about his choice of words."

"That's what I said. Then he told me pissed just meant pee. So, I guess it was okay. I'm not sure why that would make Daddy pee though. Anyway, Daddy was mad—or maybe his feelings were hurt. I told him he could help me with my Christmas tree in my room, but—"

Chase unlocked the front door. "But what?"

Heather's little shoulders shrugged as she looked up at him. "I don't think he liked the idea. He never came to help. I guess it wasn't important like all that work he has to do. Poor Daddy."

"So, is the tree done now?"

She shook her head. "No," she said softly as she removed her boots and set them on a rug for wet shoes. "Mommy doesn't know, so, please don't tell her. She'd be mad at him again."

Helping her with her coat then hanging it up, he smiled. "Hey, I got an idea. Could I help? We could pretend your dad did it if she asks."

"Would that be dishonest, Chasey?" she asked slyly.

"Absolutely," he chuckled.

"Yay! Then let's do it." Now, she clapped her hands and danced a little jig.

Chase realized he'd probably crossed some kind of ethical line with Tessa. But he figured it was for a good cause. He might be saving Robert's life. Well, every good plan had a downside. If it made the little ballerina happy, it was a win.

This Robert interference was going to stop real soon. Maybe he should have Lieutenant Ken Montgomery pay him a little visit. He'd roughed him up once and even made a threat concerning Tessa. Scared the hell out of him. The whole idea still made him grin. But the truth was, he wanted to do intimidation himself. Tessa was so scared the man would take control of the kids that she tiptoed around him, allowing him the power he still tried to use against her.

Chase was walking down the hall to maybe start some supper when he felt Heather at his heels. He looked down and stopped. "What?"

"Thank you for being there for the daddy-daughter dance today. You did a good job. Better than the other dads. I was proud of you."

"You weren't so bad yourself."

"I was actually amazing."

Chase sighed. "Thanks for teaching me. You were pretty amazing." He pinched her cheek as his heart swelled with an unfamiliar emotion.

"You think Robert will come for the next rehearsal?"

When did she start calling her birth father by his name?

"I'll let him know. Now, go upstairs and get everything ready for decorating that tree. I'm excited."

"You don't look excited."

"This is my excited face."

"I think that is your I-just-ate-a-face." She tilted her head and jammed her hands onto her waist.

He pretended to adjust his face and mouth with his fingers and finally sighed. "Sorry. This is the best I can do."

"Maybe we can work on that. I have some of Mommy's leftover wrinkle creams that can help. Does wonders for her."

Chase burst out laughing. "She does look pretty good. Think it will work on me?"

"Hmm." She tapped her finger to her cheek and smiled. "I think you might need a whole jar, so I'll see if I can find her stash."

"Why don't you just go get the decorations so we can do that tree?"

She started up the stairs.

"And, Heather," he said when she stopped at the top of the stairs and looked down at him. "You probably shouldn't mention to your mom you told me about the wrinkle cream." She gave him a thumbs-up and had taken one step when he stopped her again. "Heather."

She huffed a sound of impatience. "What now?"

"I love you."

A big smile spread across her mouth. "Well, duh." Then she ran off.

"What have I gotten myself into?" he asked out loud.

The phone vibrated to divert his attention for a few minutes while he went into the kitchen to see if he needed to put anything in the oven or Crock-Pot. Tessa was good about advance planning, and the least he could do was see if he could help.

"Speak," he ordered into the phone.

"Captain Hunter, this is Pastor Paxton. Sorry to bother you after all the work you did this morning. A few of the men say they are missing some tools and thought maybe you or one of the kids mixed it in with yours or in one of our storage sheds. I called a couple of the others, but they had no idea."

"What kind of tools?"

"The circular saw was the most expensive thing. Mostly hammers, a nail gun, some nails, and extension cords for lighting. The electrician had all his stuff and, at first, I thought maybe it got tossed in with his equipment."

"What electrician? I didn't see any electrician."

"Oh. Horace Hummer said—"

"Who? You mean that chubby guy who tried to sell me insurance on the security walk last night?"

"Humm. Well, we don't actually call people chubby anymore."

"Okay. That moron who was about sixty pounds past his healthy weight and panted like a drunk Siberian tiger? He wouldn't shut up about selling me car insurance."

The pastor cleared his throat. "Yes. Horace is very enthusiastic about his profession. He insisted the electrician took only his equipment because he helped carry his stuff to the van."

"There was no van. And I did the electrical work because the electrician was a no-show. There wasn't much to it anyway. Deacon helped me. Now there's a good guy. Worked his—" He paused to measure his vocabulary. "He worked really hard at every task he was given."

"I don't understand. Wonder who Horace helped?"

"No disrespect, Pastor Paxton, but maybe he helped himself. Ever think about that?"

"Horace tries to fit in. I'm sure he didn't—misplace the

equipment."

"We don't really call it misplace anymore," Chase said flippantly. "We call it stealing."

"Maybe I'll talk to him again." He cleared his throat.

"Let me talk to him. People tend to open up to me." His voice was edged with a threat.

"I'm sure of that. I'll keep you posted."

A scream echoed from upstairs as Chase clicked off. He took the stairs two at a time and rushed into Heather's room. She was on the floor with a four-foot white Christmas tree lying on top of her. Struggling to be free of the prickly branches, Heather fought and kicked like it was an attacking octopus.

He reached down and gently removed the tree before pulling her up. Placing it on her nightstand where the light cords dangled, he turned to see her scramble up with her bottom lip sticking out.

"Are you okay?" He motioned for her to come to him. She slowly walked into his outstretched arms. "You're safe. It's okay. Don't worry."

A tear slid from her eye as she buried her face against his shoulder. He felt her wipe her nose against his T-shirt, making him roll his eyes.

"It was an accident. I know I should have waited to put it up there, but I was anxious to get started."

He picked a few white bristles out of her hair and chuckled. "Your scream scared the life out of me. Do you think maybe you could calmly call me next time?" He switched to a girlie voice to mock her. "Chasey, I need some of your amazing assistance right now. Hurry, please. You're such a hunk."

The voice made her laugh as she wiggled out of his embrace. "A hunk of baloney maybe. I think the scream was much more dramatic."

"I agree, but you drive me crazy when you do that. Unless you want me to start calling you the Drama Queen, knock it off."

"Drama Queen?" She handed him a string of twinkly lights to place on the tree. "It has a nice ring to it. Drama Queen and King Baloney."

They went back and forth with ridiculous names until the tree was trimmed and on a timer. The joy on her face, looking at the little tree as she took his large hand with her tiny one, gave him a feeling of belonging.

She followed up by insisting he rehearse the daddy-daughter dance as she hummed the music. “You need the practice, Chasey. I mean, Chase.” She grinned.

“Okay. But don’t worry. I’m sure your dad will make it.”

Heather shrugged nonchalantly and held her hands out to start the routine. “Whatever.”

CHAPTER 11

Driving over the Sierra Mountains in a heavy snowfall did not give Chase the touchy-feely Christmas vibe Tessa was hoping to spread throughout their first Christmas together. This was yet another opportunity for the ex to circumvent his plans. The guy went cross-country skiing at a resort near Squaw Valley. Yet he didn't have a couple of hours to put up a little girl's Christmas tree.

He ran over the conversation with Tessa when she suggested he do this for her.

"Apparently, a snow plow buried his car, Chase," Tessa announced as she warmed her hands near the fireplace. I've tried to reach one of his friends to go get him. Tonight's the final rehearsal for the Christmas program, along with the last night for the live Nativity. Tomorrow is the program in place of the usual morning worship."

"Hallelujah," he mumbled.

"What?" Tessa asked, bewildered.

"I mean, I'm glad we can confine the danger zone after tonight, since there may be a kidnapper lurking in the area."

"Oh." She sounded satisfied. "Me, too. Surely, with so many people around, there won't be any problems."

"Officer Michaels sent me a text saying he'd be there tonight, and a couple of other officers will patrol the perimeter while the cookie exchange is going on. Pastor Paxton hinted the rehearsal was just a formality. The kids all knew their parts, and Santa plans to make a visit. That ought to get all those kids stirred up, considering they probably are already on a sugar high."

"Would you watch the kids, and I'll go get Robert?" she asked.

He stared at her for a few seconds, as if he'd misunderstood her words. "No, you won't. He should have never gone up there in the first place. Last winter was brutal and, for all I know, they're still digging out from the record snowfall. The guy is an idiot if he thinks he can call and have you go after him. You don't have to cater to his whims. Let me send Ken." Then he laughed. "Boy, that would be worth paying him a couple hundred dollars to go."

"Very funny." She tried to hold back her own amusement. "Maybe he could take Zoric with him."

"And Marine sergeant Tom Cooper." Now Chase choked on his words trying not to sound too hopeful for the scenario to happen. "I'm liking this more and more."

"Or maybe you could go." The tilt of her head, a sly smile, and a gentle touch to his chest were the beginning of the end for resistance.

"Why would I ever want to do that? I can't be trusted. Remember?" He walked off feeling an argument rising he wasn't sure he could win or a guilt trip he'd have for not going to get the jerk. What if the ex died of hypothermia from drinking too much punch or something? "He's not spending Christmas here. And tomorrow, we're telling the kids about us. I'm moving in, and that's that."

"So, you'll go?" she said sweetly.

"That isn't what I said."

"So, you've changed your mind?"

"About what?"

"Honestly, Chase, I wish you wouldn't lead me on like this. It's frustrating." She patted him on the buttocks. "But I love you anyway."

Tessa, one. Chase, zero.

He had long known how beguiling the woman could be, even though she pretended it wasn't true. If the CIA got wind of her ability to manipulate and whip full-grown men into completing a task with the threat of being hit with nothing more than a wet noodle and a promise of cookies, she was destined to work for a dark interrogation site in the Pacific.

And here he was, driving past the Truckee city limits sign, looking for the guy who was the number one on his-shoot-to-kill deck of cards a lot of the military guys carried in Afghanistan and Iraq. Only he wore a suit and tie with a silly grin on his face. And, to make matters even more irritating, the snow had stopped halfway up the mountain, and there wasn't much more than ten inches of snow on the ground.

He pulled over when he spotted Robert waving for him in front of a coffee shop. Maybe there would be a slick spot, and he would accidently on purpose slide up over the curb. That wasn't going to work. A support dog stood at attention next to a woman with some kind of disability, ready to step off the curb next to Robert. Just his luck.

"Hey, hon, I'm glad you made it." Robert hopped in and slammed the door before he noticed Chase was driving. His breath caught in his throat as he rubbed his hands together for warmth. "You. I expected Tessa."

"So, it seems. For a minute I thought you were calling me hon." Chase pulled out onto the street, backtracked, and headed toward the highway.

Robert gave what sounded like a nervous chuckle then buckled up.

The irritating situation was about to get worse.

"My phone went dead after I called her and—"

"You couldn't charge your phone at the coffee shop?"

"Didn't have a charger. Lesson learned." He pointed to the exit ramp onto the highway. "That was your turn."

"Thought we'd take the scenic route." Chase knew what he was planning to do was wrong, but it felt so right. "Where's your spirit of adventure?"

"Ahh, at home."

"Where is home these days, Bobby?"

"My name is Robert."

"Right. You look like a Bobby."

Robert cleared his throat. "What does a Bobby look like?"

At that moment, the SUV slid on a slick spot and fishtailed, causing Chase to let out a "yahoo." When he overcorrected, Robert tilted toward him. To keep from flopping around, he reached out and gripped Chase's leg. When Chase glanced over at him and arched an eyebrow, Robert jerked to a stiff sitting position.

"Sorry. That sudden move surprised me."

"Kind of surprised me, too." Chase felt more amused than he would have expected. Clearly, Robert was a bit nervous riding with him.

"Oh. I didn't mean to grab your leg. I feel embarrassed. Again, I apologize."

"Not the first time someone grabbed my leg."

"Yeah, but you're—you know…"

"Gay?"

Robert exhaled like a huge weight had been lifted. "Well, yeah. I mean you're kinda buff for someone who teaches French literature."

"Thanks. I try." Chase tried to appear serious. He continued to taunt the man. "You look pretty good, too. Are you seeing anyone?"

"No. No. I mean yes. The women I represent at times—oh, you know. They want a sympathetic ear."

"Ahh. Must be tough not taking advantage of a sweet situation."

Robert chuckled and straightened in his seat. "Well, temptation is a difficult thing." He stole a glance at Chase. "I'm pretty much on the straight and narrow. I'm hoping Tessa will give me another chance."

Chase swerved the SUV to miss an imaginary deer running across the road, throwing Robert against the door and popping his head against the glass. "Wow. Did you see that? That big boy was huge." He pulled his shoulders back and slowed down. "You were saying?"

"Oh, yeah." Robert rubbed his head. "Tessa. I realize now what a dunderhead I was to let her slip away. Is she seeing someone? The kids have mentioned a few guys hanging around."

"Me for one."

"Yeah. But you're, well you know."

"Gay."

"Yes. I know you're just helping out when I can't. You've worked at the university with her for a long time. I'm thinking the astronaut guy…"

"Carter Johnson?"

"Yeah. He's a known ladies' man, and he openly flirts with her whenever I'm around. Granted that's only been a couple of times, but I just wanted to punch him in the face."

"Probably should have, then," he said with amusement in his voice. "I think he's more interested in Dr. Samantha Cordova."

Robert whistled. "I can see why. Talk about one hot chick."

A quick application to the brakes propelled Robert forward only to be jerked back by the seat belt. Chase threw his arm out like a 1965 mother protecting her kids. Robert yelped as his fist slammed into his chest.

"Sorry. Reflex."

"No problem." He frowned. "So, you think the astronaut guy isn't a person I should worry about?"

Chase took a long slow look at Tessa's ex, wondering how long it would take for anyone to find his body if he went off road and…

"But I'm sure there's another guy I don't know about? She smiles all the time, doesn't get wigged-out when I don't show up for a visitation or pick up the kids. There's something going on."

"I think you're right," Chase admitted.

"Maybe you're doing a real good job." He landed a soft fist bump on Chase's arm.

"You have no idea." He cleared his throat to maintain control.

Robert's brow creased as he withdrew his fist slowly. "Maybe we should get back on the highway up ahead."

"Don't want to skip that cookie exchange tonight at the church?" Chase asked drily as he turned to use the on-ramp to the highway. "Also, it's the last night for the live Nativity. Your kids are in it."

"Are they?" He checked his calendar on his phone. "You're right. Thought it was next week. I'll try. I'm watching the old waistline. Cookies are my weakness."

"Just cookies?" Chase reached over and patted the man's abdomen, causing Robert to roughly push him away. Once more, he knew this kind of taunting was not healthy. When deployed, this always led to a stretch of rough interrogation. Merry Christmas to me, he thought.

"Hey, keep your hands to yourself," Robert snapped. "I don't need a trainer."

"Thought I'd offer my services."

"I bet," he mumbled.

Chase couldn't help but chuckle as he accelerated the car. The highway wasn't clear, although the snow was piled on the side of the road. It would be dangerous as soon as the sun went completely down. Being up here in the mountains after it snowed, melted then froze on the road would be a nightmare. The forecast called for heavy snowfall by morning up here.

The next thirty minutes were quiet until the Grass Valley exit came into view. When Chase flipped on the blinker, Robert decided to continue their conversation.

"So, do you know if Tessa is seeing anyone? You never answered my question."

"No. I can promise you she isn't."

"How do you know for sure?"

"She tells me everything. I tell her everything. I see her every day. I help out with the kids because you can't or won't. We work at the same place, in the same meeting pod, have the same friends—do I need to go on? If she were seeing—someone else, I'd know."

"I'm not into all that touchy-feely stuff. Guess you are."

He nodded without taking his eyes off the road. "I most certainly am, Bob. I mean, Robert."

"It's not like I'm ignoring the kids. I have important things to do at work. Sometimes that has to come first. I have bills to pay, too. Women are just cut out for that getting-personal stuff."

"Maybe Tessa will remarry."

"Over my dead body," Robert fumed. "She wouldn't dare. I know deep down she wants me back and is playing hard to get. Which is fine. I'll play that game if I can get her back and in my bed."

Chase came to a screeching halt in front of the law office where Robert had an apartment upstairs. He put the car in park and turned to face the ex. After a long exhale to calm his rising rage, he placed his large hand on the back of Robert's seat.

"Look, Robert. I'm not gay in spite of what Sean Patrick tricked you into believing. Tessa isn't seeing anyone else, and she won't be back in your bed, so get that nonsense out of your head before you get hurt."

"By who?" Robert huffed a kind of laugh at Chase's insinuation.

"Me. Now, get out of the car. I'd better see your ass at the church program in the morning. And you have a father-daughter dance rehearsal at three tomorrow afternoon." He reached across Robert and opened the door. "Don't make me come get you."

Robert practically jumped out of the car and slammed the door. He never looked back but hurried into this office.

"I should have finished him off when I could have dropped him from the Bay Bridge a couple of years ago," he mumbled, waiting until the man was inside before pulling away. All he wanted to do was hug his wife and spar with the kids he desperately wanted to accept him.

CHAPTER 12

Anthony Gallo drove the van he'd stolen from a Walmart parking lot a few miles from the church where Horace would be waiting for him. With a little training on the inside, he'd managed to learn a trade. It wasn't how to be an electrician, which Horace claimed they needed, but he'd become a decent carpenter. Horace was waiting and told him to go to visitor parking behind the school. True to form, he helped unload a few tools and carried them to the site where they'd rebuild the Nativity stall. There was plenty of help within the hour after he'd arrived, and he told a few who asked that Gallo was from the organization who did volunteer work for the community on the weekends.

"Heard about the trouble last night, so thought I'd come on over after Horace gave me a call. I'm also a custodian."

He was thanked several times and pretended to be busy. When Horace nudged him to spot the big guy with the two boys in tow, he decided to make himself scarce. Once, he saw the muscled guy check him out and move his way. Horace intercepted the man long enough that he managed to make his way back to the van, but not before leaving a little surprise for the evening's events. Unfortunately, when he realized he'd left the tools with his fingerprints behind, he texted Horace to bring them to him.

"I didn't remember which ones were yours, so I brought a few extra."

"Hopefully, they won't look for them before I get out of here." He chuckled. "I went inside where some of the ladies were cooking. Left some grease in a skillet. Scooped some of it up in a discarded butter bowl."

"Whatever for?"

"Spread it around the Nativity and on that tree those boys planted. Might just invite some critters to make an appearance for the Heavenly Host tonight." He snickered. "Might be just the distraction I need."

Now all he had to do was wait. Sunset arrived with heavy clouds blocking out the last rays of day when he decided he should eat. Strolling up and down Main Street, he slipped into a little burger joint reminiscent of a 1950s lunch counter with all the checkered and polka-dot patterns tourists loved.

It was the Cornish Christmas in Grass Valley. The streets were being blocked off for carolers to stroll and vendors to sell gifts for Christmas. Each little shop had decorated their windows and hoped to win the $200 prize for Best Christmas Ever award. The B&Bs were giving tours, the restaurants were packed, and musicians dressed in Victorian costumes would perform on the hour until ten o'clock.

"Ho. Ho. Ho." Horace sat down at the lunch counter next to a guy who had part of his Santa Claus outfit on. "Looks like you're missing your beard, St. Nick." Gallo could be disarming when he wanted to be.

"In my car. Parked a block away so I could get out and make my way to the St. John's Evangelical Church. Didn't want to mess up the beard before I go. A guy can't live on just Christmas cookies." This made him laugh like a jolly old elf who reminded him of the poem, so Horace laughed, too. "The kids sure will be surprised. They don't know I'm coming."

"Is that where you go to church? I'm looking for a church home myself. Moved here a few weeks ago and feel a little lost, being the holidays and all. My family is in Arizona."

"Nah, I don't go there." He chuckled. "It's called the Church of the Burning Nativity after last night." He retold the story to Anthony and nearly choked on his greasy fries in the process.

"Christmas program tomorrow, I hear. You might try it out."

They talked a while longer and Anthony paid for Santa's supper. "I insist. Not every day I get to have dinner with Santa Claus."

"Well, thank you. And Merry Christmas."

Anthony hung back far enough that Santa walked carefree, unaware of being followed. Santa stopped once to clean his glasses, and another time to watch before crossing the street. It was lucky for Gallo that Santa parked his sedan behind a closed business and a block from the action of the now-busy streets. Looking both ways as he approached the old man, Anthony pulled his collar up around his ears and his hat farther down on his forehead. When he got close enough to hear the key fob unlock the door, Anthony slipped up behind him and tapped him on the shoulder.

Startled, Santa turned around with wide eyes. "Oh. You."

Anthony's mouth stretched into a straight line as his voice deepened. "I'm not going to lie to you. I've been naughty this year, Santa."

Santa eased to the side as if he might try running away, but Anthony blocked him. "So, I'm going to have to relieve you of your stash, clothes, and money if you have any."

"I don't have any money. And those goodie bags are for the kids."

Anthony frisked him and found his wallet full of ten and twenty-dollar bills. "Now, Santa," he said, shaking his finger in the man's face. "Lying to me is going to get you a ride in the trunk." Santa tried to bolt only to be caught and slammed, chest first, against his car. "Now, let's get you undressed."

~~~~

St. John's Evangelical Church was situated on a hill above Grass Valley. The Christmas lights decorating the entire property could be seen from almost every location in the small town. There were signs along the way to help souls find their way to Sunday services each week. He didn't know how to drive on roads with a dusting of snow, so he used an abundance of caution on the way up.
~~~~

Once there, Horace waited for him at the school where he'd parked earlier in the day. This time, the lot was full because of the spillover from the church. It occurred to him how much the man resembled a penguin with earmuffs. Horace puffed on a cigarette like he was a steam engine as he paced back and forth. The guy had talked too fast and kept looking over his shoulder all day. Gallo didn't like nervous partners. Maybe he should throw him in the trunk with St. Nick and be done with it. People might miss him, however.

"Where have you been? The kids are getting squirrely. I told the pastor you were on your way twenty minutes ago."

He started to throw his cigarette in the snow when Gallo relieved him of it to finish before dropping it in the snow.

"You try wrestling Santa out of his uniform."

"Where is he now?" Horace crushed his cigarette under his boot. "You didn't kill Santa, did you?"

"Relax. He's in the trunk. The old fart had long underwear on, so he won't freeze to death."

"I'm not going to be a part of Santa dying, Anthony."

"Is my kid here? If so, show me where she is."

"She's the little redheaded kid with Down syndrome."

"Down syndrome? You never told me that."

"Still your kid, ain't it? I told you she had problems. Her adopted mom says she's high functioning."

"What does that mean?"

"It means, she can do almost anything the other kids do. Cute kid, too. Everybody loves her."

"Where is she now?" he asked, moving toward the church campus.

"Probably inside waiting for Santa like a bunch of other outlaws who have to be on your naughty list." He nodded toward the entrance. "Come on. Wait. What's that under your shirt?" He patted Anthony's chest. "You have a gun?" he fumed. "You can't take a gun inside a church. There's families and little kids."

A man materialized out of nowhere with his hands jammed into his wool overcoat. They nearly collided, when the stranger chuckled.

"Oh, sorry, Santa. I didn't see you. Where's your sleigh?" he joked. "Oh, Horace, is that you?"

"Hello, Robert. I haven't seen you in a while. I hear your law practice is doing well."

"Not bad at all."

"Stop by next week. I'd like to talk to you about some extra coverage on my kids."

"Sure thing." He grinned. "Santa, Robert here has a sweet little girl who is friends with a Down syndrome child. They take good care of each other. Maybe you could mention that if she comes to talk to you about your visit on Christmas Eve."

"Ho. Ho. Ho. I sure will. What is your little girl's name?"

"Heather. She'll be excited to see you. Still a believer. Her little friend is Kelly. They are best friends." Robert pointed his finger at Anthony's body and chuckled. "You're pretty skinny compared to last year."

"New guy." Horace grabbed Anthony's elbow and pulled him along. "The other guy has the flu."

Robert kept up with them. "Too bad. Well, if anyone asks, I'll say you've been on a diet and you plan to fill up on cookies this Christmas."

"Thanks. Now, beat it. I want to act like I just flew in," Anthony grumbled.

"Sure. I'm going in the front. Kids are practicing until you get here, I think."

Robert disappeared through the front doors of the church while Horace and Anthony went in the back door.

"Lawyer? You're friends with a lawyer?" Anthony quipped in disgust.

"You could've been more polite. You might need one if you get caught."

"Maybe I'll take his kid instead."

"Not a good idea. Remember the military guy I was telling you about? He's involved with the little girl's mom. They're divorced, and G.I. Joe is hanging around her back door, if you know what I mean."

"Might want a hostage to keep my girl calm."

"Again. Not a good idea."

Anthony halted, grabbed Horace by the collar, and shook him. "Stop telling me what I can and can't do. I thought you were all in on this."

"You didn't give me a choice."

"I think you've developed a conscience, Horace," Anthony mocked.

"Maybe I have. What are you going to do with a little girl anyway? She's only known this nice family and Grass Valley. You can't make her happy."

"Doesn't matter. She's mine, and I'm taking her. Her worthless mother had no right to give her away. What I do with her is none of your business. If it doesn't work out, I'll…"

Horace turned to see what his friend was staring at. A little redheaded girl was sitting in the Nativity singing softly to the baby Jesus doll with her parents watching with pride. The dad kissed the top of her head and hugged her.

"Is that her?" Anthony asked quietly.

"Yes. She has the voice of an angel."

Anthony watched as they led her inside. He hadn't realized how seeing her would make him feel. Strange thoughts of regret and loss nearly choked him at hearing her little voice sing "Away in a Manger." The way she took her adopted dad's hand and giggled at whenever he spoke to her made his heart lurch with jealousy.

"It's not too late to back out of this, Anthony. She is well taken care of."

"She's mine, and I'm taking her with me. Now, if you aren't up to helping me, I'll let the people in high places know how your insurance operation is a fraud game. Don't give me the holier-than-thou routine. You're no better than me."

Horace frowned, giving a submissive nod. "No gun play." They entered a small vestibule. An older man followed them inside, and Anthony froze when he greeted them.

"Horace. Santa," he said pleasantly before walking through the door to the recreation area of the church.

"I know that guy," Anthony whispered to Horace as he disappeared.

"Who. Him? How could you know Deacon."

"His name isn't Deacon. It's Flynn Fitzgerald."

"You're mistaken. He was here when I came. Retired. Helps out at the Old Time Mercantile Kelly's dad owns."

He chuckled. "Well, what do you know. Guess you and me

aren't the only ones with a secret."

"What are you talking about? That guy is as clean as they come."

"Not so. He's my girlfriend's father. Turned her against me. Time for a little payback."

"Are you saying he's Kelly's grandfather? Why would he be in hiding under a false name?"

"A good question."

CHAPTER 13

The rehearsal was short-lived, comprising of a few songs with hand gestures and how the children should march into the worship service the next morning. Since a number of parents were watching, the choir director didn't want to give too much away. The children were delighted to discover they would be excused for family fun in the recreation hall.

Robert stood in the back of the sanctuary watching when Chase came through a side door, not far from the stage. With his arms crossed on his chest and a face void of emotion, he reminded him of a bouncer at a dance club. Not that he'd ever been to one. But he'd seen movies. The man often scanned the area and once landed his eyes on him, raising his chin in a greeting. The man gave Robert the shivers.

Their conversation of a few hours ago still irritated him. What was he talking about concerning Tessa? It sounded like the man wanted him to stay away from her? So, he wasn't gay or what? How could he have gotten that wrong? He remembered a time when he mentioned it to Tessa. She had laughed then said she was pretty sure that wasn't the case. Why did Chase always watch him like he was a piece of meat for a pack of hungry lions?

Come to think of it, the guy was rather sinister and shady.

Maybe he'd check into his past when he got home tonight. The thought of Agent Dennis Martin of the FBI came to mind. The agent got him out of a tight spot once, which ended up making him look like a hero. That was good for business. Chances were good he could run a thorough background check on him. Maybe the Mr. French Literature was just overprotective of Tessa since they worked together. She would never fall for a character so crude and rude.

The guy came across as a junkyard dog to him. He certainly didn't want him around his kids, especially Heather, who was incredibly trusting and gullible. She'd inherited that trait from her mother, not him. One thing for sure, he could read people pretty well, and that Chase character was a mixed bag of secrets and no good. He could feel it in his bones.

Suddenly, Tessa walked out the side door and stood by Chase. He uncrossed his arms and smiled down at her when he said a few words, making her laugh. What could such a moron say to make Tessa giggle like a schoolgirl? The most disturbing part was how she gazed up at him as if he was a rock star. She reached over and patted his chest gently as he slipped an arm around her shoulders. Their attention was diverted to him when Heather waved in the middle of a song.

Trying to appear cool, he raised his chin in a sullen greeting then waved back to his daughter. At least Chase knew he was here and removed his arm from Tessa's shoulders. Most likely intimidated that he knew what he was trying to pull. The decision was made to call Agent Dennis Martin now. He wouldn't be surprised if he was a felon hiding in plain sight. Why hadn't he noticed that before? Probably had tattoos over his entire body. Come to think about it, all those friends Tessa had accumulated in the last few years were a little sketchy—except Dr. Samantha Cordova. She was a goddess.

Before he could pull out his phone, the children were dismissed to their parents. Heather and Daniel came barreling toward him. Sean Patrick was nowhere to be seen.

"Dad, you came." Daniel gave him a high five.

Heather hugged him around the waist the best she could.

"Of course. Didn't want to miss any of the fun, especially the cookies. Where is your brother? Isn't he in tomorrow morning's program?"

"No. But he is King Herod at the Nativity. Too old for this one."

Tessa and Chase joined them.

"He's out at the live Nativity. I'm sure he'd love for you to say hello." Tessa was her usual sweeter-than-pie self to demonstrate what a fool he'd been to betray her. Was she using that ogre standing with her to make him uncomfortable? Besides, since when did she need a bodyguard? "The kids were hoping you could make it tonight."

Robert tousled Daniel's hair and patted Heather's cheek. "Of course. Wouldn't miss it. Tradition. Right?"

"Right," the kids echoed with gusto. Each took one of his hands and tugged.

"Let's go. Pastor Paxton said there would be a surprise." Heather jumped up and down in her usual fashion. "I bet it's Santa."

"I bet you're right. I think I even saw him earlier, headed this way."

"Really?" Heather gasped.

"There's no such thing as—" Daniel stopped when Chase reached out and laid a hand on his shoulder. "I mean, we'd better go check things out." Daniel turned Robert's hand loose and stepped closer to Chase. "You're coming, aren't you, Captain?"

Chase grinned and gave him a wink. "You bet, buddy."

Daniel leaned in to him and put a hand on the ogre's waist instead of the high five he'd given to him. But he quickly withdrew and stole a quick glance at Robert then motioned for him to hurry. "You coming?"

"Let me make a quick call. Wait right here. Just take a minute." He called Agent Martin and was surprised to hear he was in Grass Valley. He quickly turned from his kids to tell him he wanted information concerning Captain Hunter then clicked off. "Let's go." Robert frowned at Tessa who had walked ahead with the ogre. What was she thinking having that bruiser around the kids? "Tessa, I want a word with you before you leave." Did she take the ogre's hand?

"Sure. I'll be here all evening. Part of the cleanup crew."

"Want any help?" Robert came alongside her, making a point

to ignore Chase.

"I'll be around to help out," Chase interjected before Tessa could respond.

"Won't you be on security outside?" Tessa asked.

"Right."

Robert smiled internally. She'd just blown the guy off. "Maybe we could talk then."

"That would work, Robert. Thanks." She smiled.

That moron could think whatever he wanted, but Tessa just made it possible for Robert to be alone with her. His spirits immediately lifted as they entered the chaos of the recreation hall. Several people gave him a shout-out, and he saluted them as he followed Tessa and Chase to a few seats.

The man called Deacon came up to Chase then acknowledged Robert. "Long time no see, Robert." He glanced toward Tessa then appeared to remember they weren't together anymore as he turned his attention to Chase. "Your turn on the security walk. I promised to pass out the stocking treats after the kids get to talk to Santa. Mrs. Sharp also informed me I'm down to help Pastor Paxton with crowd management."

"Not a problem. I want to make sure there's smooth sailing around the Nativity anyway. Get many visitors tonight?"

"Actually, we did. Guess they were curious about the excitement last night." He grinned. "I think they were surprised at how fast we put things back together. Quite a few came inside for chili dogs and cookies."

Robert held up his hand. "What happened? I was in Truckee."

"Robert went skiing with a few friends," Chase added.

Deacon laughed and gave him a quick version of the excitement.

"And our boys were involved?" His tone was a cross between shock and irritation as he leveled a dangerous glare at Tessa.

"Not only were they involved, they assisted in the sacrifice. The original baby Jesus was decapitated by the fire department when they hit it with a blast of water." Tessa grinned mischievously.

"It's okay though. Pretty sure it was holy water," Deacon laughed.

Chase smirked and shifted his narrowed glance at Robert who

didn't appear to think the story was funny. "But you'd be proud of the boys. They came back today and helped rebuild it for tonight. They even took their money to buy a Christmas tree we planted out by the Nativity."

"Did the pastor say anything about a new Santa tonight?" Deacon's smile faded.

"No. Why?"

"One came in, and he isn't our usual guy. Skinny and smells like cigarette smoke. He's with Horace."

"Oh, yeah. Met them outside before I came in," Robert interjected. "Kind of cranky to be Santa. Not friendly at all. They were coming from behind the school."

"Really?" Deacon asked. "We always provide a parking place right outside there." He pulled back a curtain to look at church staff parking spots. "Takes the pastor's slot because he has a bad hip. He won't let us pay him, so we try to get him as close as possible."

"Not sure about that, but mentioned the usual Santa had the flu and couldn't make it," Robert informed them as he waved to Ellen, the pastor's wife. "Boy, she's put on a few pounds."

"Robert," Tessa gasped. "Be nice."

"I talked to him on the phone two hours ago and offered to bring him myself. He didn't say anything about being sick." Deacon scratched his head.

"Tessa, I'm going to go check on things outside. Deacon, will you touch base with Santa's wife and make sure he really is ill." Deacon gave a thumbs-up and headed off to a quieter place.

"I'm going to round up the kids and keep them close." Tessa scanned the crowd.

"I see them. I'll bring them over." Robert gave her arm a squeeze.

Chase eyed Tessa as her ex moved into the crowd. "He thinks you're getting back together."

"Are you implying I'm giving him that impression?"

"You have given him that impression because he thinks I'm gay and no threat to him getting you back in his bed." He spoke out of the corner of his mouth as he surveyed the crowd.

"I want you to know. When he was in my bed, he wasn't in

my bed. Understand?" Tessa slipped her hand in his, which always managed to defuse him. "But it's kind of sweet that you're jealous."

"Tessa..." He sighed and decided not to attempt reasoning with her. "Do you know the willpower it takes to keep from loading him up on a C5A Transport Plane and dropping him into Afghanistan?"

She stepped closer and whispered in his ear, "I most certainly do."

He pulled his head back to gaze into her eyes twinkling with mischief. "It's a good thing I love you."

"Yes, it is. Otherwise, I'd have to load you onto a plane with him and drop you in Afghanistan. Now, go do whatever you're supposed to do and rescue me from Robert's attempt at reprimanding me for being such a terrible mother. I'm sure it's going to come up since he knows about the fire last night." He'd stepped away when she grabbed his sleeve and pulled him back. "By chance, did you threaten Robert today on your way back from Truckee?"

"Me?"

"I thought as much. Wanted to be prepared when he brings it up."

"I just got a text message a few minutes ago from our favorite FBI agent. Apparently, Robert wanted him to do something about me."

This brought a laugh from Tessa, causing several people to glance her way. "Like what?"

"Investigate me, I think. See if I was a felon or maybe a terrorist. Who knows? Just so you know, he's meeting me outside in" —he glanced at his watch— "five minutes. I'm sure he's going to have a good laugh over this."

"What?" Tessa gasped. "Agent Martin can laugh?"

"Keep it up. I understand he's coming dressed as the Grinch to match his mood. Oh, and he has more information for Kelly's parents. Wants to talk to them ASAP." He leaned in to kiss her then thought better of it when he spotted Robert staring at him. When Ellen Paxton stopped Robert to chat, Chase sent a narrowed gaze and elbowed Tessa. "Your name is mud now, kiddo."

"I'm going to have to do something about her, too, aren't I?"

Tessa sighed as she caught the woman's eye and finger waved to her. "Bit—"

"Tessa," Chase snapped. "Watch your mouth."

"Go," she demanded, giving a hitchhiker thumb sign toward the door. "Here comes Santa."

CHAPTER 14

Chase walked briskly toward the exit door leading out to the Nativity. He toyed with the idea of stopping Santa to check him out. But before he could, Pastor Paxton was standing next to him, shaking his hand and laughing at the jolly old elf. Since he didn't act overly concerned, Chase hurried outside to check on Sean Patrick.

"Where've you been?" Chase asked the kid as he approached with a spray bottle in hand.

"Oh, Luther said his dad thought it would be nice for folks to come outside and watch the live Nativity one more time since we'll all be together. He sent a bottle of bug spray in case there were mites on our tree. Afraid they could bite the actors."

"Mites?" he asked skeptically. "Let me see that?" Chase took the clear bottle and recognized a sweet, minty fragrance when he sniffed it. "Why doesn't it have a label? And why didn't Luther do this instead of handing it over to you?"

"Mrs. Murphy makes organic spray, so it wouldn't hurt the tree or the kids if they got around it. Smells nice."

"Okay. Then, why didn't Luther do it? We've discussed not trusting him."

"His mother came to get him. Said he wasn't supposed to be

hanging around me, so he forced it into my hands while she was looking away and hurried off." Sean Patrick shrugged. "Since Kelly was out here, I didn't want her to get bitten. I didn't get any on me. I promise. Old Mrs. Murphy is really into lots of organic stuff. She's like a witch or something. Mom goes to visit her all the time for stuff in her garden. I figured it was okay."

"A witch? Perfect," he moaned.

Sean Patrick gave a sinister smirk. "Yeah. Mom's been feeding you stuff for a long time. I think she got it from that old witch."

"Probably the same baloney you've been feeding me. I had a little chat with your dad concerning me not being gay."

"Oh good. I'm glad you cleared that up." He was backing away when Chase lifted his arm to stop him.

"Sean Patrick, I'm not trying to outdo your dad or take you from him. I love your mother very much. I want her to be happy, and I want you kids to have the kind of home where you feel safe. I know you have issues with your dad leaving, but—"

"I don't have issues with my dad leaving. I have issues with you trying to take his place. I was doing fine taking care of us. I don't need another one of him. He hurt my mom and us."

Chase narrowed his eyes at the kid who now stood taller than his mom. "I'm here to stay, Sean Patrick, whether you like it or not. I'm in for the long haul."

"Good luck. I know you think you're a kind of knight in shining armor to my mom, but it's all in your head. You aren't the only batter in the game." He pushed past Chase and stomped through the snow. Before he opened the door, he turned back as if to see if his competition was still watching. He was.

What the heck was he talking about? Another batter in the game? Was he talking about his dad or someone else? The thought occurred to him Sean Patrick would be a good fit with the Secret Service intimidation or profiling department. How old did you have to be to start work?

Chase moved toward the Nativity and told the few kids putting things away they needed to go inside. The games and talks with Santa were starting. "I think all the visitors will come back out to watch your last performance in a little while."

"Thanks, Captain Hunter." One boy gave him a high five.

"Sean Patrick sure is lucky to have you around."

"Why is that?" He learned the things Sean Patrick shared might be a twisted version of the truth.

"He says you're always teaching him cool stuff like tracking, hunting, and self-defense. Told us his batting improved after you gave him a few tips." The kid kicked up snow with the toe of his boot. "My dad is great, but he doesn't know anything about sports. Maybe you could teach me those tips in the spring so I can make the team?"

"Maybe your dad would like to help me."

"Really? That would be awesome, Captain Hunter. Thanks."

The boy ran over to tell a couple of the others. There was a lot of head bobbing and turning heads his way.

"What's that all about?" It was Officer Michaels from the Grass Valley Police Department.

"I think I've been elected batting coach for their team in the spring."

"Be aware their mothers think they are on the fast track to the major leagues. They only won two games last year, and one team didn't show up on time from Auburn, so that one was a default." He snorted a laugh. "Because they're a church team, everyone kind of takes advantage of them. They might as well be Amish."

The boys walking to the door to go inside waved and gave him a thumbs-up. "Maybe I'll change that," he said. "Sean Patrick is a good hitter. Daniel is coming along on his catcher skills. Now all we need is a little badass mentality with the others."

"Well, if you can beat the Baptist team, you'll earn that reputation. Those kids are monsters when it comes to playing baseball."

"I've already signed up to coach Heather's team."

Officer Michaels choked. "What? You?"

"New league for girls. Already got my team together."

"Pray tell, what is your team's name?"

Chase took a moment to survey the area as he pulled back his shoulders. "I was going for The Bombshells."

"But you ended up with what?"

"The Unicorn Sparklers." He grimaced.

"You're killin' me," Michaels laughed.

"Yeah. Well, you should see the shirts they picked out. And if you keep laughing, I'm going to make you my assistant coach."

Laying his hand on his heart and taking a deep breath, Officer Michaels motioned for Chase to follow him across the road to the school parking lot. "Okay. I'm done. We have work to do. A call came in about ten minutes ago about noises coming from the area behind the school and thought we should check it out. We don't need any more surprises."

As they sloshed through the wet snow, Chase recognized Agent Dennis Martin's dented car coming down the street. He decided to let him deal with the inside of the church. There were two other officers patrolling nonchalantly around the perimeter. Not much ever happened here in Grass Valley, at least nothing like an escaped convict wanting to kidnap a child. He hoped they were on their game tonight.

One of the streetlights flickered in the back parking lot of the school and another one was out. Officer Michaels made a note to call it in to the street department come morning. The lot was full. Each man took a section to check for irregularities. Besides a few cars taking up more than one space and another parked in a handicapped spot, nothing appeared to be out of order until they met up on the back row.

"Hear that?" Officer Michaels whispered as he shone his light up and down the row.

Chase moved toward a faint thumping. "Over here." He touched the inside of his coat where he kept a small handgun holstered securely.

With each step they took, the sound grew louder. "Under those trees over there. Edge of the lot. No one parks there because it's a tight squeeze. Must have been the only spot left." Officer Michaels took out his weapon.

"Someone is in the trunk." The car rocked with each thump. Chase walked to the driver's side and used a rock to break the glass. After finding the trunk release, he rushed back to open it as Michaels leveled his weapon.

The flashlight beam zeroed in on the inside of the trunk. Both men shifted their gaze to each other then back at the man dressed in his long-handled underwear. With duct tape across his mouth and his hands tied behind his back, the man had managed to kick out the taillights. While Chase freed him of the tape and helped him out of the trunk, Michaels called for an ambulance.

Chase helped the visibly shaken man sit in the back seat with his feet on the ground. When the ambulance arrived, the paramedics took over and wouldn't let Chase or Michaels have any contact until he was checked out. They moved him to a gurney inside the ambulance, but he was sitting up, sipping a bottle of water.

"Sir, do you know who did this to you?" Officer Michaels asked.

"Yeah. A guy who wanted my Santa outfit."

Chase's whole body went on alert. "Santa outfit? Were you supposed to be Santa for the church tonight?"

He nodded. "Yes. Been doing it for years. The guy followed me from the diner. And—"

Chase and Officer Michaels took off running back to the church at breakneck speed.

~ ~ ~ ~

Heather's little hand slipped into Tessa's as the cookie contest began. Families always competed to see who had the best decorated sugar cookies. She was sure a few of those moms were on Pinterest a little too much considering how beautiful the designs were. They were supposed to team up with their children to enter four sugar cookies to be judged. From the looks of them, the moms had done the bulk of the decorating. Not her bunch. Her kids each had a cookie to decorate, and she was still finding colored icing and sprinkles in the kitchen. She'd let Chase decorate cookie number four for them since cleaning up the mess looked like a job for a hazmat crew.

"I know we'll win this year, Mommy. I know it." She squeezed her hand.

"The families did a great job." Tessa smiled at her as Sean Patrick came to join her with Daniel in tow. Robert followed.

"Daddy, I think we'll win. Chasey helped us and-"

Robert's head jerked up then he glared at Tessa. "Chase? Why didn't you call me? We always do this as a family."

"I did call you. I believe you decided to go skiing," she offered sweetly through gritted teeth. "Remember?"

"The captain has a lot to learn about cookie decorating." Daniel elbowed his brother. "Right, Sean?"

"He did okay." He shrugged. "How was the skiing, Dad?"

"Well, that was a surprise I wanted to show you, but it didn't work out. I didn't really go skiing. I bought us a new van. Has all the bells and whistles. There's TV screens for you guys to watch videos when we travel." He put his arm around Daniel's shoulders. "The skiing story was to keep the secret. Well, I might have skied a time or two. I traded in that old truck I had and—"

"You mean the one you said you'd save for me when I turn sixteen?" Sean Patrick asked, bewildered.

"Yeah. Well, you got a few years yet. I wanted something we could travel in."

"How about your Lexus?" Sean interrupted.

"This will have more room. Besides, that is more of a work car." He fist-bumped Sean Patrick's arm. "I thought we'd take a trip to Yellowstone. Camp. Fish. You know, take in the sights before it's too late."

"Too late for what, Daddy?" Heather chirped.

"For us to go as a family. Right, Tessa?"

Sean Patrick cocked his head and let one corner of his mouth lift. "I'm sure Mom will love that. Right, Mom? Hey, maybe Chase would like to come. He's all about roughing it."

Robert dropped his arm from around Daniel's shoulders. "Why don't you guys go find us a place to sit before the winners are announced for the cookie contest. I see they're serving hot dogs and chips. Help your sister with hers. I want to talk to your mother."

CHAPTER 15

Tessa's children got in line for hot dogs while she silently counted backward from one hundred. Whatever was in Robert's craw, it was going to make her look bad and him a rock star—just like always. Caution was the rule of the day, since he knew enough ins and outs of the law to make her life miserable.

"Can you believe how big Sean Patrick is getting. He's taller than me now," Tessa sighed. "They aren't babies anymore."

"And you've done your best to keep them that way," he snorted.

Tessa cut her eyes to him, her jaw flexing in impatience. "What do you want to talk to me about, Robert? Can't it wait until after this party?"

"I guess so." He sounded bland and wouldn't face her. "It's just—I don't think I like that Chase guy hanging around you guys. I'm concerned."

"Why are you concerned? He's great with the kids, helps me out all the time because we both know how busy you are. He's a gentleman to me, his students, other children, and the neighbors. As a matter of fact, the Ervins next door think of him as a son. They've known him for years."

"I don't like it."

"Which part?"

"I think he believes I'm out of the picture and there's no chance of us getting back together."

"There is no chance, Robert." Tessa turned her cold eyes on him. "I don't care how many vans you buy, how many trips you say you'll take the kids on, you and I are finished. We both know why, so stop pretending this wasn't your fault. It totally was, and there's no going back."

She'd stepped away to leave when he reached out and stopped her. "Tessa. Please. You're right, I know that. I was a cad and took you for granted. I want to do better."

"Then, show up for Heather's rehearsal tomorrow."

"Rehearsal?"

"Daddy-daughter dance. She asked you weeks ago. It means a lot to her. You are coming to the recital on Monday night, aren't you?"

"Of course," he stuttered. Chase had already reminded him of the rehearsal. "I thought it was next Monday, but yeah, I'll be there."

"And the daddy-daughter dance?"

"I'll try."

Tessa rolled her eyes.

"Yes. I'll be there. Text me where to go for rehearsal. I may not be able to pick her up."

"And tomorrow's program? In the morning. At eleven."

"Sure. Sure. Sure. Of course."

Tessa wanted to make a harsh comment concerning the lack of Christmas enthusiasm, but he never had embraced the holidays until she'd completed all the work. Like a Christmas miracle, he would say how much fun it all was, and next year he'd help more. He never did. But, for now, a figure coming through the door caught her eye, making the children squeal with delight.

It was the green Grinch from the beloved book and movie. The walk, the gestures were perfect. Tessa couldn't stop laughing until she had to cover her mouth and nose to keep from snorting. A tear squeezed from her eyes as she loved this surprise immensely, knowing this was no easy task for the man inside the suit. The pastor grabbed the microphone and taunted him a bit until the Grinch took it away from him and complained with his own dialogue.

When little Kelly ran up to him and shook her finger and demanded he say Merry Christmas, he did a little protest dance, making everyone laugh. But, in the end, he gave in and spoke deeply into the microphone.

"Oh, all right," he fumed. "Merry Christmas, you bunch of rugrats."

There were a few good-natured boos laced with giggles and taunts, but it was all in fun. He told them after they had talked to Santa, they'd better come get their picture taken with him, or he would take the old fat boy's sleigh for a ride without him. More boos and laughter continued as he strolled among the tables, making his way to Tessa.

Tessa bent over laughing and pulled the Grinch in for a bear hug. "I so love you right now."

The Grinch pretended to stroke her hair and roll his eyes then leveled one of those mean scowls at Robert. "She is so needy." He mimicked the Grinch's evil smile then shifted his attention to Robert as he changed his voice to normal. "What was so important I needed to be here, Mr. Scott?" came a familiar voice.

"Agent Martin?" Robert gasped. "Is that you?"

"No, imbecile, it isn't me. Do I usually look like a Grinch?"

"Oh, Dennis, I didn't think you'd actually do it. You are amazing." Tessa grabbed him around the waist again and this time kissed him on the nose.

"Stop it," he ordered. "You'll ruin my makeup." He pushed her away. "What did you want to talk to me about, Scott? Be quick about it. I got people to harass."

Robert started to move away to a quiet corner then motioned for the Grinch to follow him. The bushy eyebrows of the Grinch lifted in obstinance as he put his hands on his hips. "Tessa, I hope you're happy. I've been reduced to this, thanks to you. I hope my debt is paid in full now."

"What debt?" Robert asked. "You guys know each other outside work? I thought you met when I got into—"

"Trouble with the conflict diamond market?" Agent Martin bent down to let a mom take his picture with her son then winked at the mom. "No. Tessa didn't tell you? She lets me sleep on her couch from time to time." Another evil grin. "Is that what I was supposed to say, honey?"

Tessa burst out laughing again. She wasn't sure her amusement was because Dennis was such a good actor or the horrified expression on Robert's face. Heather was the frosting on the cake when she ran to him and he swung her up in his arms.

"Hey, you." She patted him on the cheeks with both hands. "Are you going to sleep with my Barbie doll again tonight. I won't let her goose you like last night. Mommy says I need to pick up my toys better."

The Grinch growled a reply. "I took all your toys and threw them in the dump."

"Mommy, is that true?" she asked in a skeptical voice.

"I think Agent Martin is teasing you," Robert said matter-of-factly.

"I am not," he insisted. "I hate toys. No one gets toys this Christmas, Santa," he yelled across the room.

"Put me down this instant, Grinch." She pushed her face into his. "I mean, Uncle Dennis." She smiled with more pats to his cheeks.

"Hmmm. Okay. I'll go get your toys from the dump tonight. You're such a brat."

"You're such a fibber. I'm adorable. Mommy says so all the time."

Sean Patrick and Daniel walked up and nodded to the Grinch. "Agent Martin. Good job, man." Sean Patrick gave him a thumbs-up and handed him a plate. "Here's a hot dog for you."

"What is going on?" Robert ran a hand through his hair.

"I owed Tessa a favor…"

Tessa cleared her throat.

"A favor or two," he corrected. He gave her a sneaky expression. "But I need another night on the couch."

"But not with my Barbie." Heather shook a finger at him.

"I pulled her head off, so we're even."

Heather huffed and stormed off, pretending to be irritated. "Fine."

"Get on with it, Mr. Scott. I got things to do." Agent Martin raised those green bushy eyebrows again in a show of impatience. He nodded to an open spot over by the wall. "We can talk over there."

Robert glanced around as if afraid he might be watched. "Did you find anything out about Captain Hunter?"

"You mean, did I dig up any dirt on him?"

"Yes," he insisted. "That guy is sketchy."

"Very much like your ex-wife, Captain Hunter has the ear of the president and a number of other people in the government. He's a decorated Army Ranger, and Delta Force officer who served in Afghanistan. Not so much as a speeding ticket. Teaches the yawn-worthy class of French Literature in the Renaissance Era and speaks several languages. Never married and—"

"Because he's gay, right?" he asked quietly.

This caused the agent to choke back his laughter. "Humm. No. He's quite the ladies' man, I hear. Why do you want to know?" The agent followed Robert's line of sight where Tessa was playing with Kelly and Heather at one of the game tables. "Oh, I see. You think he's playing patty cake with the ex."

"I'm not sure." Robert sighed. "Maybe."

Agent Martin twisted his Grinch mouth into another evil smile. "Let me reassure you. He is."

"What? How could that be?" Robert gasped.

"Hell, look at her." He pointed to Tessa causing several kids to wave back at him. He blew them off by crossing his arms across his chest and stuck his nose in the air, which delighted them. "Cute as a bug with a bit of a tarnished halo, but not rusty—yet."

"What are you talking about? Tessa is just—Tessa."

"Yeah. Exactly. Your ex-wife has the world by the tail, and no one is trying to get away."

"Including you, it sounds like." Robert's tone was indignant.

"Ha. That's none of your business. Anything else?"

"Can't you—I don't know—make this problem disappear?"

"Look, I did you a favor once, but I won't again."

"It was your job. I had been abducted and tortured in some location when you showed up."

"I have no memory of that," the agent lied coyly as he took a finger to rub his forehead in confusion. "What I remember is illegal trafficking of conflict diamonds by the law firm you were working at. We had you red-handed as being involved. If you hadn't cooperated, you'd be getting handmade Christmas cards from your kids in a six-by-eight cell in a maximum-security prison back East."

"Then why did you come here tonight, if not to bring me information about Hunter and help me?"

"The information I gave you was what I already knew about Hunter. Well, he's a pain in the you know what, too. A lot like you. I'm here because Tessa asked me to do this Grinch thing, drove me around today because my car was in the shop, let me sleep on her couch, fixed me breakfast, and thinks I'm an old softy. Which I'm not, by the way. That little girl of yours..." He paused. "She is yours, right?"

A pained and confused expression came over Robert's face.

"Never mind. Anyway, she calls me Uncle, which, I guess, makes me practically family."

Robert frowned and started to walk away, but the agent stepped in front of him.

"A word of advice about Hunter. Don't mess with him. He has a long fuse but will burn your ass if you get in his way, threaten Tessa, or ignore those kids." The agent smiled and patted Robert on the arm. "Other than that, he's a real charmer." He pivoted and waved to a couple of ladies with their heads together who took turns sending him a coy smile. "You, there. Are you talking about me?" He gave the typical Grinch expression and scooted their way. "Get your cameras ready, ladies!"

CHAPTER 16

The Santa appeared to be taking his time with the children. The pastor had requested the parents to wait until later to take pictures since they might run short of time. Tessa walked with Heather to stand in line to speak to him and was grateful they secured a place behind Kelly's mom. Both little girls held hands, giggling about what they planned to say. Kelly waved to him each time he glanced her way and made sure to offer an exaggerated wave of his own.

Tessa continued to observe him closely since something felt off. He didn't match up as a jolly old elf. She could smell cigarette smoke from where she stood. There was a hint of a five-o'clock shadow on places the fake white beard didn't cover. To top it off, he was skinny and not much taller than her. Of all the Santas she'd seen in her life, he was the worst. He also did a lot of head bobbing and, whatever the child asked for, he would say, "Of course, you can have that. I'll be sure to put it under the tree for you."

A couple of parents tried to soften the blow coming on Christmas morning by suggesting what Santa meant was if he had room in the sleigh. But Santa would wave the parent off and say, "Don't pay any attention to them. I'll make room. Just be good until Christmas."

To add insult to injury, Santa invited one of the teenage girls if she'd like to come talk to him and patted his knee. True to form, she called him a pervert and pulled her little brother away after her. The teen became animated when telling her father who then cornered the pastor. He glanced toward Santa and leveled a stern expression. The pastor rubbed his forehead and his face turned red, Tessa searched the crowd for Deacon. Hopefully, he had a few answers about sick Santa.

Much to her horror, she heard one of the kids walking past her say Santa's breath smelled like his grandpa's happy juice. Knowing who his grandpa was meant the happy juice was a whiskey and soda water. She leaned in to Kelly's mom and whispered her concern and, thought since Kelly's welfare may be at stake, she suggested taking the girls to a different part of the room. As they started to leave, Santa called out.

"No leaving before you talk to old Santa. Come here, little girl." He motioned for Kelly who jerked away from her mom and ran to Santa. She quickly climbed up into his lap and, for once, the Santa gave a child his undivided attention.

Maybe she'd misjudged him—but that thought faded when he called her Kelly. How did he know her name?

"Mommy, you're hurting my hand," Heather complained, trying to pull free.

"Kelly," her mother called softly, "it's time to go back to the Nativity. We need to get ready," she lied.

"Okay." She jumped down. "Bye." Santa hugged her and kissed her on the cheek.

Tessa didn't like it. He hadn't shown any other child that kind of attention.

Her mother hurried forward to intercept Kelly and led her away.

"My turn." Heather looked up at her mother. "Why do I have to go?"

"It's your time to be Mary at the Nativity." She noticed Daniel and Sean Patrick were already headed out the door to take up their positions.

"Where's Kelly?" Deacon asked, coming alongside her.

"Over there. Did you reach your friend's wife?"

"A neighbor answered. Said she was on the way to the

hospital. Her husband had to go by ambulance. Maybe he really was sick. Hope it wasn't a heart attack." He gazed toward the new guy and froze.

"What is it, Deacon?" Tessa couldn't help but see the look of hatred fill Deacon's eyes as they narrowed. "Are you okay?" Silence. "Deacon, do you know this Santa guy?"

"Yes."

The cookie coordinator distracted her with the announcement of the awards for best-decorated cookies. Winners won a basket of goodies from a local food market plus a gift certificate to a greenhouse. Before she could quiz Deacon further, he hurried to Kelly's parents to speak to them. Whatever he told them, their eyes widened, and Kelly's dad gathered her up in his arms.

"Pastor Paxton said he wants everyone to go out and watch the Nativity play to conclude the evening." It was Robert, munching on one of the winning cookies. He grinned. "I got to pick the best. Ellen and Kelly's mom tied." He waved the cookie. "Ellen is in a huff, is all I have to say about that. She thinks you put me up to not choosing her. Are you two on the outs? She seems like such a nice lady. Not!"

Her thoughts were not very Christian at that moment. Where did she put her voodoo doll?

The crowd lumbered toward the exit. Deacon held one door open, while Horace held the other. Deacon still wore a sour face and kept watching each person as they went through. Although people were friendly, saying thank you for holding the door, and Merry Christmas, Deacon merely nodded and gave a straight-line smile that gave the impression he might be in pain.

"Are you okay, Deacon?" Tessa asked as he reached down and patted Heather on the head.

"Yes." He gave Heather a piece of soft peppermint candy. "I know you'll do a great job tonight."

"Kelly did good, too. She and I both played the part of Mary."

"I know. Proud of you both."

Heather beamed and ran out to take her place for the play.

Tessa stole a glance at Horace who appeared to be sweating in spite of the cold night air hitting him in the face. He kept stretching his neck to peer back inside the main hall. She followed his line of sight only to see skinny Santa moving through the cookie line. It appeared Ellen Paxton followed him while shaking her finger in his face, complaining about his manners.

"Tessa, come on." Robert touched her elbow then slid his hand to her back to give a quick rub. "The boys want to show us the tree they bought."

While people were finding seats on hay bales, camp stools, and a few folding chairs, others stood on the sides to watch the short rendition of the first Christmas. She noticed the children in the play lining up outside the corral. The two lambs wore collars and leashes held by Daniel who had dressed in his shepherd costume. Several other boys followed holding their noses and complaining about a smell. Sean Patrick had slipped into his purple robe and crown and ordered the other players to straighten up. He took his part seriously.

"Sean Patrick is pointing to the new Christmas tree they bought." Robert leaned in close enough she could smell his aftershave.

"Is that tree leaning a bit?" Tessa tilted her head. "I thought I saw something move."

"The wind has picked up. Probably needs the ground stomped down to compact it better."

The mom standing on a ladder near the lean-to structure, who held a flashlight high over her head to represent the star, waved it like it was Obi-Wan-Kenobi's light saber. Her screeches put everyone on edge.

"I don't remember this part of the Christmas story." Robert chuckled.

"Shut up, Robert. Something is wrong." Tessa watched as the woman's husband ran to the ladder that was tilting to try and stop it from hitting the ground. Two others ran to help. They all threw up their hands and yelled.

"Get out of here."

"Shoo!"

"You nasty thing."

Chaos ensued the next few minutes as men ran hunkered over chasing a shadowy creature. With the sound of whistles and slapping hands together, two men collided, and ended up on the ground. When they tried to scamper up in a show of dignity, they managed to look like a tube man in front of Jim's Tire and Lube.

The kids were laughing at the dads until several raccoons lumbered out with an unknown lump in their mouths, followed by a possum the size of a house cat. The moms standing along the parade route jumped onto nearby chairs, which flipped over spilling them into slushy snow.

Skinny Santa had joined the crowd and laughed so hard he wheezed. "Guess someone dumped grease after fixing that chili today."

He continued to laugh until Pastor Paxton and Ellen joined the crowd.

The children's minister waved to the pastor and made the okay sign with his fingers. The parade and play commenced with prerecorded Christmas music, the crowd singing along.

Tessa tried to put space between her and Robert, but he stepped closer, rubbing his arm against hers. With anxious anticipation of Chase appearing out of nowhere, she scanned the area in case she was forced to circumvent any confrontation between him and Robert. She glanced up at Robert who returned a pleasant smile as if nothing had changed between them. When he lifted his hand to her back, she took a step away and frowned.

"What are you doing?" she whispered.

"Sorry. This is such a special moment, watching our kids in the live Nativity, the snow— everything. I miss you." His voice turned quiet and sentimental. "We didn't get to talk. Can I come over tonight?"

"No," she growled. "It will be late. I've still got to clean up for services tomorrow. I said we'd talk then if I can. Now, pay attention."

Robert huffed his displeasure but refocused on the parade of children.

Once in the lean-to structure built earlier in the day, the children recited their parts, adding in a couple of songs. Applause followed as Agent Martin came to stand next to her. He appeared taller in such a ridiculous outfit. Standing silent, he kept turning his head as if in search of a problem, or maybe he was bored and couldn't wait to be gone.

As the last song concluded, Ellen edged closer to the new Christmas tree planted on the edge of the lean-to. Apparently, turning on the lights to illuminate the tree had been forgotten.

When the pastor's wife connected the electrical cords, it burst into a blinding blur of white twinkle lights. The tree began to vibrate, and a loud howl emitted from deep within the branches. Ellen raised her hands to block her face and screamed when a ball of black leaped from inside the tree onto her body. Between her terrified cries and the black cat's screeches, the tree exploded into billowing smoke.

"Look out!" several men yelled as they ran forward. This time, they were prepared with fire extinguishers and reduced the tree to a white foam mountain of waste.

To add to the chaos, kids were running like scared rabbits, and parents scrambled to nab their little actors while others rushed back to watch the mayhem unfold in a kind of humorous display of Murphy's law. The excitement was over almost as quickly as it began. Except for Ellen who fought the black cat on the way down to the ground. She displayed a graceful backward splat into a collection of sheep nuggets piled to keep the area clean.

Pastor Paxton rushed to her rescue, only to get in the path of the runaway cat and the fire extinguisher spray. In spite of jumping away from most of the spray, he still managed to take on the appearance of a melting snowman who may have peed down the front of his pants. As he pivoted toward his wife, he hit mushy snow, throwing up his hands in a hallelujah gesture.

Tessa wasn't sure how it happened, but an echo of gasps escaped several church ladies as the pastor landed on top of Ellen's lower body. He splattered wet snow when his knees dug in alongside of her hips and his face planted in the middle of her chest. She tried to push herself up when the pastor finally managed to lift his head and speak in an irreverent voice.

"For heaven's sake, Ellen. Lie still so I can do this."

This, of course, added to the comedy of errors as the men tried to resist laughter and failed. Amused at the situation, Robert and Deacon raced forward to assist Pastor Paxton to a standing position. He reached down and jerked his wife up into his arms and grinned boyishly at her. Perhaps a little taken aback by his wolfish grin that her husband displayed, she giggled like a schoolgirl.

The black cat rubbed gently on the pastor's pant leg and purred. The feline hissed at Ellen when the pastor lifted it into his free arm. Irritated, she jumped aside. Mrs. Murphy came running up with the bottle of spray Sean Patrick used on the tree. She snatched the cat away from the pastor.

"Oh, my poor Black Magic," she cooed, loving on the cat.

"Black Magic?" Ellen snapped. "Do you think that is an appropriate name, Mrs. Murphy?"

"Oh, shut up, Ellen," the pastor growled. "It's a lovely name."

"Well, this"—Mrs. Murphy waved the bottle— "was sprayed on the tree. I can smell it. The bottle was lying on the ground."

Tessa approached. "What is it?"

"Catnip. I make it for Black Magic as a treat. I keep it in a bottle on my porch. The label has been pulled off."

"Was there a reason you brought it tonight, Mrs. Murphy?" Tessa reached out to the cat who welcomed the scratch behind the ears.

"Well, it was in my trunk when I brought in supplies for tonight. I left it open because my hands were full. I guess a volunteer took it out thinking it was part of my things. I live only a few houses away and it was too far for me to carry things up that hill, so my kitty must have followed me or sniffed the catnip."

Luther came slinking up and reached to dust off the chunks of sheep pellets from his mom's coat but recoiled, wrinkling his nose. "I saw Sean Patrick spraying the tree before I went in earlier."

Robert pulled off part of the string of lights then brought it over to the others. "Looks like your cat chewed through the lights. I guess when Ellen plugged them in, it shorted out." He chuckled. "This Nativity scene is jinxed."

"Well, it figures Sean Patrick was involved," Ellen huffed.

Before Tessa could react, a familiar squeal echoed near the back of the stage area. It was Heather. She turned to see her daughter run out of sight, her cries fading into the darkness. Her brothers appeared to be rolling on the ground fighting until she realized they were trying to stand.

"Boys, where is your sister?" she said, jerking them up by the arms. Sean Patrick had a face full of snow, and Daniel rubbed his head as if dazed. "Boys!"

Sean Patrick staggered and had started to bolt into the woods when Tessa grabbed him by the shoulder. "Heather," he cried, his voice panicked. "Mom, he took Heather and Kelly."

"We tried to stop Santa, but he had a knife." Daniel's costume was sliced open. “He cut me, Mom.”

Tessa could feel a scream beginning to escape from deep inside her.

Chapter 17

No doubt that scream belonged to Heather. Nobody could let out a bloodcurdling scream like that pint-size little girl. There had been a couple of times Chase had warned her not to be so dramatic, but now he was glad she hadn't taken his advice. What had terrified her?

He accelerated, leaving Michaels to follow. Knowing trouble had found his family, Chase's endorphins kicked in. He reached the perimeter of the outdoor staging area. People were in chaos, calling their children, a smoldering tree was covered in a white substance, and Tessa stood in a fighting stance that meant Ellen Paxton was predestined to have a hell of a shiner for Christmas.

Next, he watched her running, shouting Heather's name in the panicky voice he'd come to know over the last few years. In one quick scan, he spotted Sean Patrick and Daniel being held back by their father. Kelly's mom was crying hysterically, and her father was on the ground, bleeding.

In a weird kind of moment, Chase spotted the green Grinch throw off part of his costume and pull his weapon as he ran toward him. He was staring at the woods near the church and called out to Chase.

"They ran into the woods, Chase. Santa took Kelly." Agent

Martin ran past him.

"Go," Kelly's mother insisted as she kneeled down by her wounded husband where a church member came to help him.

"Where's Heather?" Chase caught Tessa's arm as she ran up to him.

"She's with Kelly," Mrs. Parker cried. "Oh, my heavens. That monster took the girls."

Chase gave Tessa a guarded look. "Stay here. I will get the girls. I promise you." He saw the pain in her eyes. "You know what to do, babe. Be strong." The boys ran to him with the look of hopelessness in their faces. He put a hand on each shoulder. "Are you all right?"

"Yes, sir," Sean Patrick said bravely, even though his quivering bottom lip said otherwise.

Tessa bobbed her head like a toddler and touched his arm. "Be careful. Don't shoot the Grinch. It's Dennis."

Officer Michaels called for backup and followed Chase into the woods. He relayed the message to dispatch that the green Grinch was FBI and tried to catch up.

~ ~ ~ ~

How could two little girls be so slippery and heavy, Gallo wondered? His daughter was hysterical and cried so loud into his ear he squeezed her a little too hard, causing her to gasp. The other pint-size monster was screaming and hitting him in the head with her fists. She blinded him for a few seconds with a sock to the eyeball.

The sudden disorientation caused him to slam into a tree, dropping her. No matter. He still had Kelly. She wasn't a fighter like that other kid that would draw attention to him. He used his foot to push her over into the snow, but she bounded up to her knees when Kelly reached for her and repeated her name multiple times. "Heather. Heather."

"Shut up. You're coming with me," he grumbled and plowed forward.

Something slammed him in the back, and he stumbled forward to get a better footing. When he turned slightly, another snowball smashed into his nose then one to his forehead, staggering him backward. Kelly managed to wiggle free just as he heard voices calling for the girls. The first child ran to Kelly and pulled her into the woods. In seconds, they'd disappeared, but the male voices grew louder. Time to escape. He slid down the hillside to the car Horace had left for him and could see the Grinch emerge from the woods, gun raised and aimed at him. It must be the FBI agent who dogged his every move. Time to take care of that problem once and for all.

The Grinch made it down the hill and jumped into the street, aiming his weapon just as Gallo floored the car. The car fishtailed so that the front missed the agent, but the back bumper thumped him down. Thoughts he'd injured the man dissipated quickly when several shots broke out his back window. There was no time to turn around and finish the job since he probably wasn't alone. Instead, he picked up speed and headed toward his next pickup location.

~~~~

The screaming stopped several minutes into the search. Had the girls been taken to a rendezvous meet with another person waiting? Were they hurt? Chase's heart pounded so hard, he thought he'd collapse from the fear that gripped him. Hearing a car engine start as he came near a side road in a quiet neighborhood, Agent Martin yelled out his location then ran toward the car.

Chase made it there as the dark sedan peeled out and sideswiped Agent Martin. He managed to jump back but was still pushed off his feet. The car disappeared down the street, around a curve before they could get a license plate number or the make.

"Over here," Officer Michaels yelled. The two men tore through the brush toward his voice and came to a halt when the officer held up his finger to his lips. "Listen."

"It's okay, Kelly. It's okay," came a small familiar voice.

Heather.

Tears formed at the corners of his eyes and his heart impeded him speaking in a clear voice. "Heather!" he choked over and over. "Heather!" Then she was running to him, calling his name until he scooped her up into his arms.
~~~~

Two more ambulances arrived at the church, along with the fire department and most of the police department. Pastor Paxton was comforting the people and told them to go back inside the recreation hall because the police would want to talk to them. They could stay busy by getting the hall ready for services or going into the sanctuary to pray for protection for the little girls. He had the children's minister help with parents and brought out games and a movie to settle them down.

Tessa was pacing back and forth when Robert approached, frowning at the people around him. She didn't want to deal with him right now. Both the boys grabbed her and held on tight, giving her a much-needed distraction.

"Mom, where's Heather?" Daniel had tears running down his face, mixed with snot that he quickly wiped on his sleeve of the shepherd costume. "I tried to save her. We both did."

"Chase and Agent Dennis went after her, sweetheart." Trying to sound calm, she peeled open his costume, relieved to see he wasn't bleeding. She pulled his head against her.

Sean Patrick stood rigid and put his arm around her to hold tight. "Mom, he'll bring her back. Don't worry." He kissed her cheek then leaned his head against hers.

"What in the heck is going on, Tessa?" Robert joined her and turned his head to look around at the chaos. "Was that Heather screaming? Where is she? What happened to Kelly's father? Good Lord, there's blood all over him."

Deacon walked up, holding Horace by the collar, his hands fastened behind his back with a zip tie. He pushed him down on the ground in front of Kelly's parents. "He was working with that creep playing Santa."

"I didn't know he was going to shoot Kelly's dad in the leg. I didn't," Horace begged.

"If anything happens to that child, I'll kill you." Deacon had taken on a hoarse, dangerous tone. "You knew he had a gun."

Another officer arrived and took Horace to a squad car. Tessa reached out to Deacon and told him to go with the Parkers to one of the ambulances. "Could you go make sure things are okay? I know others are doing that, but you are always helping them, and they trust you with Kelly."

"Don't worry, Mr. Deacon, sir. Chase will bring her back. You tell the Parkers that," Sean Patrick insisted. "You'll see."

Deacon reached out and laid his hand on his shoulder. "Thanks, son. I'll tell them."

"Again. Where is Heather?" Robert fussed.

Tessa tried quickly to explain the problem and the possible danger Kelly was in and how, even though they tried to have protection in place, unexpected things occurred.

"Great. You let our daughter go into harm's way with a child, a family, who posed a danger to us. How could you?" he snapped. "I'm going to go look for her," he announced as he straightened his coat and pulled on his gloves. "Which way did she go?"

"Dad, let Chase handle it," Daniel begged. "He might shoot you accidently."

"What? He carries a gun?" he shouted in horror before turning back to Tessa. "Did you know about this?" He held up his hand. "Don't answer that. You're still making irresponsible decisions concerning the children. I can't trust you with them anymore."

Sean Patrick's nostrils flared as he pulled back his shoulders and stared at his father. "Don't talk to my mom that way. I don't like it."

"Really? Well, you got a few things to answer for concerning last night and tonight. Seems to me you aren't getting enough discipline these days. Just running your own con game on your mom so she'll take up for you with no accountability."

"Stop!" Tessa snapped. "This isn't the time to discuss my parenting skills. Heather is what's important right now."

This caused Robert to clamp his mouth shut and nod in agreement as the gravity of the situation hit him. "I'm sorry. You're right. What can I do?"

Pastor Paxton slipped a hand on his shoulder. "Pray. That's what everyone is doing inside the sanctuary. We'll get through this."

Shouts came from the men who waited outside to help clean up and secure the area. "They're coming back. Can we get more light out here?"

Tessa rushed forward as several flashlights shone into the woods. The person she saw was Officer Michaels, the arm of the Grinch around his shoulder. He was limping but appeared to be okay. Then Chase appeared behind them carrying a little girl in each arm.

"He got them," the cheer went out. "They're here!"

Tessa burst into tears seeing both little girls clinging to Chase with their arms around his neck and their heads on his shoulders. Robert stepped forward, visibly relieved at seeing them. Kelly's mom ran to intercept them as they broke through the woods. Grabbing her child, she wept, thanking the three men through garbled tears.

"Thank you, Chasey." Kelly smiled as she let her mother pull her away. "I wuv you."

He reached out with his free hand and patted her cheek. "I wuv you, too."

As they moved toward the ambulance to be checked out, Tessa fell against Chase. He wrapped his free arm around her. She laid her head against Heather's body and sobbed.

"It's okay, Mommy. The Silent Knight rescued me." Heather smiled and patted her mother's head. She had given him the name after he retold how the song "Silent Night" came to be written.

"I see that. He's pretty good at that kind of thing." Tessa gazed up at him as he tried to wipe her tears away.

Tessa's boys came up and timidly hugged the three of them, making a point to caress their sister tenderly.

Robert pushed up and put his hands on Heather's little waist to pull her free of Chase, but she frowned and tightened her grip on the soldier. The gesture surprised Robert causing him to take a step back. Although relieved, Chase knew hes would be irritated at the rebuff.

"Tessa," Robert began as Chase adjusted Heather on his shoulder.

"Heather needs her mom right now. Anything you have to discuss can wait until tomorrow after morning services—if that's okay with you." Chase leveled one of those steely glares, said to be able to stop a charging elephant in his tracks. "Is. That. Okay. With you?"

Sean Patrick mimicked Chase's glare and easily removed Heather from Chase's hold. She grabbed onto her brother like a lifeline.

Robert glanced from Chase to Tessa, who was in no shape to argue. She kept reaching out and touching Heather, asking if she was okay. "You're right. Maybe we should take her over to the ambulance to make sure she's not hurt."

"Good idea," Chase agreed as he moved toward one of the ambulances.

He let Robert walk alongside Tessa, not sure of how much to enforce his growing annoyance with the man. Daniel and Sean Patrick took up positions on each side of him, trying to match his long strides.

Sean Patrick cleared his throat. "Guess you really are a knight in shining armor." He tried to joke but failed as Chase dropped a narrowed gaze on him. "And I'm sorry about what I said to you earlier."

Chase waited as he turned his head to make eye contact with the boy.

"So, are we good?" Sean Patrick jumped in front of him and stopped.

"We're good." He raised a fist for the boy to meet with his own. "What happened to the tree?"

"Sean Patrick sprayed catnip on it. And Mrs. Murphy's cat chewed the electrical cord. Mrs. Paxton ended up with sheep poop in her hair." Daniel grinned.

Chase burst out laughing as he put an arm around each boy's shoulder and started off again. "That should be a good story. Let's go take care of the girls first."

Chapter 18

It was after midnight when Chase pulled into the driveway with his family in tow. The boys staggered inside, and he carried Heather to her bedroom with Tessa following. He heard the boys knocking around, getting ready for bed, followed by their mother telling them good night and how much she loved them. Landing a kiss on the little girl's forehead, he comprehended how lucky they had been tonight. This could have ended so differently if not for this brave little girl trying to save her friend.

"Chase, I think Officer Michaels pulled into the driveway. He might want help with our Grinch." She stood leaning against the doorframe of Heather's room.

He slipped his arm around her waist and pulled her tighter against him as she reached across his abdomen to snuggle close.

"I'm going to check on the boys, then I'll go downstairs to help Michaels."

"Okay," she whispered then moved to fuss with Heather's covers. "I'll be right there."

The boys must have fallen asleep immediately, given the soft snoring coming from the room. He didn't understand this feeling of belonging or how he could be proud of such small people who went out of their way to make him crazy. Was this another kind of love? What made this helpless, overprotective impulse that overwhelmed reasonable expectations of order in his life? There was no rhyme or reason to this kind of love. No reward. And there it was. He loved these kids.

He felt Tessa's hand on his back and turned and followed her downstairs.

"Dennis, how long are you going to wear that makeup?" Chase asked as Officer Michaels led the agent inside carrying a cane someone had decorated with white-and-red stripes.

"I'm not sure. Those women at the church kind of thought I was hot. What kind of kinky stuff goes on there, Tessa? Are you in a cult I should know about?" he grumbled, pushing past them and headed toward the kitchen. "I never got a thing to eat all night, except that hot dog, thanks to your parade of nonstop interferences."

"I'll scramble you some eggs." Tessa patted him on the back causing him to turn and smile mischievously at her. "And bacon, too?"

"Don't push your luck, Grinch. I'll bring out the attack Barbies if you aren't careful."

"Humph." The agent found a seat at the island as the other two men joined them. "How's Heather?"

"Still upset, but for Kelly mostly. Apparently, Kelly had overheard her parents talking about a possible kidnapping then shared it with Heather. So, when that Santa grabbed her and took off, Heather began screaming to get everyone's attention. When people froze, she followed, thinking she could save Kelly."

"Well, she was very brave." Officer Michaels reached for the cookie plate. "I guess when she got close enough, she threw a snowball with a rock in it that hit him in the head. He dropped Kelly, slipped on a patch of melting snow, and tumbled down the incline that goes down to Sutter Lane where he had a car parked. He must have heard us calling for Heather. We were getting close by then. If she hadn't done that, Kelly would be long gone."

Tessa shivered and covered her mouth, letting a tear trail out of one eye. "I'm so scared right now."

Chase handed her a cup of hot tea. "Deacon recognized the skinny Santa after he got there when he made the mistake of readjusting his beard," Michaels added.

Tessa passed a plate of eggs and bacon to Dennis as he explained a few things. “No way of knowing for sure, but we think Gallo also recognized Deacon and hurried up with whatever he was planning. When the Christmas tree exploded and all eyes were on the comedy unfolding with Ellen Paxton, the attention was off the girls. It was the perfect distraction, and he ran to get her. But Mr. Parker knew what was happening and tried to intervene. Gallo disabled her dad with a knife to the upper leg, not a gun as Horace thought. So much was going on, no one noticed.” Agent Martin shrugged. “Well, of course, I noticed, being a such fine Special Agent of the FBI.”

“You feds are all alike. Toot your own horn whenever you get a chance.” Michaels rolled his eyes.

“And you locals are all alike, too. Whine. Whine. Whine. I mean, until you want your problem solved the right way.” Dennis began to sound like his alter ego, the Grinch, again.

“How did Deacon play a role in this, Dennis?” Tessa poured him a cup of coffee. “Oh, it’s decaf.”

“I hate decaf. Why are you torturing me?” he snapped then grinned at her. “Anyway, turns out, Deacon is Kelly’s biological grandfather. His daughter ran away from home with Gallo. When she realized what a mistake she’d made and was pregnant, she tried to reconnect with her family. But it was too late because she’d passed away. Fortunately, she’d left him the information about the Parkers adopting Kelly. He tracked them down here and befriended them but never shared who he was. Kelly is everything to him, and he cried as he told the Parkers the truth and how sorry he was at the deception. He couldn’t bear to lose Kelly and her parents.”

Tessa stood with her hand on her heart and her lip quivering. “That is so touching.” She swooned. “What did the paramedics say about you, very special FBI Agent Martin?” She poked him in the side with her finger. “How long are you sleeping on my couch?”

“Rolled my ankle and got a few bruises when I fell. I’ll go to the doc when I get back to Sacramento in a few days. Besides, this is Christmas week. No way I’ll get in to see a doctor until after Christmas. No worries though. I’ve already made reservations at a hotel. I want to find this guy before he tries anything else. He’s an escaped felon, and I intend to get him.”

A knock at the front door jerked them to go on full alert. The men pulled their weapons and approached the door as if they were ready to kick in a hideout for the Taliban.

"Robert!" Tessa gasped as Officer Michaels swung open the door and jumped backward with three powerful guns aimed at him. "What are you doing here?"

With weapons now holstered, the men stepped aside and let him inside, although his concern clearly showed on his creased brow. "What is going on? Is everything okay?"

"Yes. The children are in bed fast asleep. Officer Michaels brought Agent Martin since there was—"

"No room in the inn," Agent Martin mocked. "Did I get that right?" He bent toward Tessa, kissed her on the side of the head, and gave her a side hug. "I'm going to bed, Tessa. I'll make myself at home, like always. Thanks for the eggs." He pivoted and limped off.

Officer Michaels tried to hide his amusement but failed as he choked a goodbye. "Hmm. We'll talk more tomorrow. Get some rest. We have a car parked out front of your house. Same with the Parkers. Chase, I assume you'll activate your security system." Chase nodded and gave him a sidelong glance of amusement as he walked the officer to the door. "Night."

Closing the door, Chase turned to stare at Robert who glared at him.

"Aren't you leaving, too? "Robert's brow pinched in confusion.

"Nope." Chase walked off toward the kitchen, leaving Tessa and her ex alone.

"Tessa, I want to talk now."

She motioned toward the living room off the foyer. A fire burned in the fireplace with a push of a button. The lights of the Christmas tree clicked off as they sat down.

"I saw all the lights on and thought I'd better stop to make sure you were all right."

Tessa sat in an overstuffed chair near the fire. "We're fine. What do you want to talk about?"

"There seems to be a parade of men coming and going here." He glanced down the hall and spoke quietly. "Are you seeing Agent Martin? Isn't he a little old for you?"

"I'm not seeing Agent Martin. Most of the time he doesn't like me. He is just in rare form tonight. I think it's the costume. He got hurt in the process of chasing down the kidnapper and I don't want him to be alone. After all, he did you a favor once so…" Tessa took a deep breath and let it out slowly. "Anyway, I'm not seeing him. He's a person I work with once in a while when I deal with the State Department in DC. Kind of a contact."

Robert cocked his head as if he didn't believe her. "What about Mr. Muscles? Are you seeing him?"

"Robert, are you here to interrogate me about my personal life because, if you are, then stop. You have no right to tell me if I can or can't see someone. And if you are trying to control me by using the children as a pawn, you need to think twice about that."

"Okay. Okay. But I am concerned about the kids."

Tessa blinked as if she were bored. "The kids are always my top priority. You used to tell me all the time how annoying it was. Now you think that's changed?"

He put his face in his hands as he leaned forward.

"Robert, it is late. I'm tired. And I want to go to bed. Chase is staying to make sure we are safe from Gallo, although I don't think he's interested in us, only Kelly. He has no idea who we are. But, to be extra careful, Chase and Agent Martin are here."

"What can I do to help?" He propped his forearms on his thighs. "Please."

"You can come to the kids' music program in the morning then take Heather to dance rehearsal tomorrow. You haven't practiced for the daddy-daughter dance, and the recital is Monday night. You signed up for the dance, and Heather is counting on you."

"I'll be there. Promise. Anything else?"

"Don't be so hard on Sean Patrick. He's a kid, no matter how big he looks."

"He needs a firm hand."

"He needs a father who is there for him."

"Well, you kind of took care of that, didn't you?" he accused. "Now this Chase guy is hanging around acting like he owns the place and you."

Tessa stood and walked to the door. "Good night, Robert. I'll see you tomorrow." When she opened the door, a police officer was standing against the railing.

"Jeez." Robert flinched. "You scared the life out of me."

"I wanted to make sure things are okay before I go back to the car."

"Thanks, Tyrone. Mr. Scott was just leaving. Agent Martin and Chase will be here all night, so we are well protected."

He nodded and ran down the steps.

"Tyrone? Are you on first-name basis with the entire police department?"

Chase came up behind him and cleared his throat. "Thanks for stopping by, Robert. Trust me." He grinned at Tessa. "I got this."

CHAPTER 19

Dawn broke to a dreary sunrise. A heavy blanket of gray clouds let the sun peek out for short periods of time, and the temperature had risen enough to start the snow melting. Tessa's roses still bloomed on the south side of the house and had not suffered from the unexpected December storm. They rarely had enough to last through Christmas, but the hope was this time would be different. Up in the mountains, the snowpack was plentiful, and anxious skiers had been hitting the slopes for five weeks.

Tessa hurried down to the kitchen with Chase having left her bed an hour earlier in case the kids got up. Although they had eloped months ago, it was still a big secret outside of Enigma. Chase had firmly planted himself in their lives to get the kids used to him always being around. It made her love him more than she thought possible. Finding him making pancakes for the crowd, she slipped her arm around him, and he bent to give her a quick kiss.

"I think Heather is up. I heard her humming in the bathroom." Tessa yawned and poured herself a cup of coffee, which she held with both hands to keep warm.

"She came down a few minutes ago with a surprise for Agent Martin, aka the Grinch." He raised his chin toward the family room where the agent slept on the couch.

Tessa took a peek inside and sloshed her coffee when she saw the agent, one leg on and one leg off the couch, surrounded by about twenty Barbie dolls. "Did she place those, or did you help?"

"I had nothing to do with that. She said it was important he have good medical care so she brought Doctor and Nurse Barbie. I'm not sure what all the others are, but I'm sure he'll appreciate them staring at him when he wakes up. He'll probably scream like a little girl."

"No Ken doll?"

"Apparently, Ken is on duty at the FBI since Agent Martin is indisposed. According to Heather, he volunteered to fill in for him."

"That was good of him." Tessa dared take a sip of the brew.

"My words exactly. Here she comes. I'm sure she'll want to see his reaction."

Tessa wrinkled her nose. "Me, too!"

Heather staggered in and fell against her mother. After setting her cup down, she picked up her daughter like she was three again and walked into the family room.

Agent Martin stirred, stretched, and moaned.

Heather wasn't shy about the volume when she spoke. "He's kind of noisy in the morning, isn't he, Mommy?"

"Yes. I'm betting he's still a grouch, too."

Without opening his eyes, he grunted. "I can hear you. I'm not asleep."

"All of us came to be with you, Uncle Dennis." Heather used her singsong voice.

He opened one eye and turned his head toward her, sending Astronaut Barbie tumbling to the floor. With the movement of a sloth, the agent turned his head toward his chest and sleeping area filled with Barbies. He jumped as if Tased, sending the world of Barbie in several directions. The girls laughed as he struggled to get off the couch.

Chase, still in the kitchen, didn't try hiding his laughter. "I am totally creeped out," he complained as he rubbed the cobwebs of sleep from his face. "Do all of these belong to you?" He shook a finger at Heather who giggled and ran to sit next to him.

"Yes. Would you like to play Barbies sometime?"

"Sure. How about two years from today at 7 a.m. if it snows

three feet?" Agent Martin agreed.

Heather stuck out her hand. "Deal."

The agent grinned and gently shoved her aside after shaking on the deal. "Feed me, you brat."

"I'm the Sugar Plum Fairy, I want you to know. It's from The Nutcracker. There aren't any brats. Will you come see me dance?"

"Do I have to pay for a ticket? Because I'm not paying to see a bunch of kids I don't know, dance."

"It's free, but you still need a ticket."

"Count me in."

"Goody. You should see Chasey dance. He practiced with me when my dad couldn't make it. On the night of the dance, all the dads get to wear a kind of pink tutu over their shirt and pants."

The sound of a pan hitting the kitchen floor indicated this may be news to Chase.

"Is that right? I'd pay to see that," he said loud enough to wake the dead.

"Heather, get your brothers." Chase came in waving a spatula. "Tell them Agent Martin might eat their share if they don't hurry it up."

As she scampered away, the FBI agent laughed at Chase. "I'm getting a mental picture of the mighty Captain Hunter in a tutu."

"And one of the parents snapped a picture of you running around with gun drawn looking like the Grinch who stole Christmas. That will make good conversation at the Bureau."

"Touché."

The Sunday service was uneventful. The church was packed more than usual. Whether it was due to the musical program or the gossip or because there were always unexpected surprises happening at St. John's Church, was not known. The local newspaper showed up hoping for a story. It was announced the annual Christmas dinner would be served Wednesday night and guests should be sure to bring a person in need. Food baskets would be available in the morning, and volunteers to hand them out in the parking lot would be appreciated.

After the service, Pastor Paxton stopped Tessa and wondered if she and Sean Patrick could come to his office for a couple of minutes. Chase said he'd take the other two children with him and meet her at the car. Since Robert was a no-show, there was no need to think about including him.

Walking inside the office, Tessa admired the walls of books and a few pictures of his family. It was a side of the pastor she didn't often think about. But, seeing Ellen rise from her seat and Luther sitting with his legs stretched out like a bored sloth gave her pause.

Tessa suspected she was going to have to bite her tongue to keep from exploding, or would the police be called to haul her off to jail for what she wanted to do to the woman?

"I appreciated your short message this morning, Pastor Paxton," Sean Patrick said, crossing his hands in front of his body.

"Why, thank you, Sean Patrick. Which part did you like best?"

"Mostly the short part." He grinned.

Tessa could feel her face flash hot, but the pastor laughed and agreed.

"You'd be surprised how often I get that request. Glad I could make an impression." He shifted his focus to his sullen wife. "Speaking of impressions, I think Ellen has a few words to say to you two. Ellen?"

Ellen glanced at her son. "Get up, Luther," she growled. "Now."

He exhaled then stood, shifting his weight to one hip.

"What have I done now?" Sean Patrick narrowed his eyes at Luther.

Ellen cleared her throat. "Hmm. Several boys saw Luther pass the bottle of catnip spray to you last night. After he told you it was to kill tree mites so no one would get bitten, you sprayed the tree heavily."

Luther frowned as he shoved his hands in his pockets. "Sorry, dude. I was being a jerk."

"Thanks, man." Sean Patrick extended his fist, and Luther quickly bumped it with his own.

"And what about you, Ellen?" Tessa asked in a vindictive voice.

"What about me?"

"You owe my son an apology, too. Not for just last night, but the night before when it was your son who was smoking and making fun of Kelly Parker. Even called her a retard."

"I'm not sure all of that—"

"Ellen, do it!" the pastor said hotly.

"Sean Patrick, apparently, I was remiss and jumped to conclusions as to your guilt."

"Say. It," Tessa hissed.

"Sean Patrick, I'm sorry I accused you of being a delinquent. I know now it was my son." She leveled a dangerous gaze toward Luther and sighed. "That it was Luther. I'm deeply sorry."

Sean Patrick nodded his head politely and looped his arm through his mom's. He backed her toward the door. "Thanks, Mrs. Paxton. You're okay. Not near as bad as everyone says you are."

As her mouth flew open, Tessa and Sean Patrick hurried out of the office toward the nearest exit to the parking lot. Laughter escaped so quickly they could barely catch their breath.

"What was that all about?" Chase asked as they buckled in.

Sean Patrick repeated the scene, causing his brother and sister to laugh, too.

"Your heart was in the right place." Tessa turned to look back at him.

The pizza they ordered for lunch arrived as they pulled into the garage. When the doorbell chimed, the kids went thundering into the house. Daniel threw open the door before Chase could stop them. Fortunately, it was the delivery kid and not a menacing character from his past.

"Guys, your mom and I want to talk to you about something." Chase felt his heart skip a beat. The Taliban never made him feel like this. "Tessa, why don't you go set the table and make a salad, then we'll come help eat that pizza."

She gave him the okay sign and mouthed, "Good luck.

"Is this another one of those don't talk to strangers speeches?" Heather chirped happily. "I already know all that."

"Then why did you take off after that weirdo last night?" Daniel asked his sister.

"I didn't actually talk to him. I was trying to save my friend." She stuck her bottom lip out and wrinkled her brow. "I—"

"Okay. No. That isn't it." Chase held up his hand. "But Daniel is right. Next time, wait for us when you want to be a hero."

She gave a thumbs-up. "Got it. Can we go eat now?"

"No. There's something else. It involves you guys, and I want your advice. Well, maybe your approval is more like it."

"Oh, brother." Sean Patrick connected with Chase's gaze and leaned back on the couch, crossing his arms across his chest. "The pizza is getting cold so hurry it up, Knight of All Things Heroic."

"Then let me talk, Knight of All Things—"

"Roguish." He smirked. "I kinda like that. The Rogue Knight."

"What about me?" Daniel tapped his jaw and rolled his eyes upward as if pondering the possibilities. "Knight of Courage and Wisdom. How does that sound?"

"Oh, I like it," Heather encouraged. "Sean Patrick, pick another name. I don't know what ro-gush is."

"Not ro-gush. Geeze. Roguish. You know kind of a rascal or trickster."

Daniel snickered. "It also means scoundrel."

"Okay. Can I be a knight?" Heather asked enthusiastically.

"No. Girls aren't knights. Maybe a princess." Sean Patrick reached over and tickled her. "How about Princess Can't Mind Her Own Business or Princess Bossy Pants?"

"Humph. I'm thinking Princess I'm in Charge of All the Knights?" A sly grin appeared as she jumped on Sean Patrick and tried to kiss him which he fought to avoid unsuccessfully.

"The longer you keep me from talking, and I know that is your goal, the colder the pizza gets," Chase said. "Makes no difference to me. I like cold pizza. I had to eat a lot of cold food when I served in Afghanistan, and—"

Sean Patrick sighed. "So, you're just wanting to tell us more war stories? Haven't we heard all of them?"

Knowing these three were trying to trip him up toward a total meltdown gave him a new appreciation for what happened to terrorists he interrogated during his military service. No wonder they spilled their guts after a few hours. He counted to ten three times before his hard glare managed to silence their nonsense.

"I wanted to tell you how much you mean to me."

The three of them grew unusually quiet and scooted closer together.

"Are you leaving us?" Heather asked softly.

"No, Heather. I'm trying to tell you—ask you about me staying for good. I love your mother so much and want to marry her. You guys are part of the package I'd be marrying, and I want you to be okay with that. I understand you don't know me all that well, but I promise I'll do the best to make your mom happy and be a responsible stepdad."

The silence was deafening. Was this another trick to make him squirm? If it was, then they were doing a good job.

"Do you want to ask me any questions?" Chase tried his best to be unafraid and calm.

Heather tilted her head, took a big breath, and let it out slowly. "Does that mean you'll be staying the night, every night?"

"Yes. Unless I have to go out of town for my job with the university—like your mom has to from time to time."

"We don't have any more bedrooms, Chasey." Heather wrinkled her brow in concern. "Where will you sleep?"

Okay. We're going down that rabbit hole, he thought. "Maybe your mom and I could share a room. That's what married couples do." He dared cut his eyes to Sean Patrick who stared at him with zero emotion. Daniel began toying with the edge of his sweatshirt.

"Does my daddy know about this?" Heather asked in a serious tone. "I don't know if he'll like you sharing a room."

"Maybe not, but he isn't your mom's husband anymore. He'll always be your dad, and that's okay with me. But I want you to know I plan to work hard at being responsible for you guys. You already mean the world to me."

"We need to talk about this," Daniel announced and slid off the couch. "Could you give us a minute?"

Chase stood. "I. Guess. So." Man, these kids were tough. He strode out into the foyer. What if they said no?

He watched them whispering and nodding. Mostly Heather did the talking, using her hands to make points then rolling her eyes upward or huffing when Daniel tried to interrupt. Sean Patick mostly stood there, occasionally peeking around his little sister at Chase with a Grinch smile on his mouth. That couldn't be good. Heather ran out to him then put her hands on her hips.

"We have another question, Chasey?"

"Shoot," he said.

She motioned for him to bend down. "Will you and Mommy have a baby? I would like a baby to fuss over. I used to be the baby, and now I'm all grown up, and I want a baby. Can you make a baby?"

Chase stood up to his full height of six foot one and glanced at the boys who were giving him the evil eye. “I would be open to negotiations concerning said baby.”

“That sounds like a yes.” She held up one finger for him to be quiet and wait before running back to the boys.

They huddled up, and he couldn’t tell how it was going since all he heard was mumbling. In a quick turn, they approached him. Why did he feel like a wounded impala on the Serengeti with a pride of lions headed his way?

Sean Patrick gave his siblings one last nod then eyed Chase from head to toe. “I guess we’re okay with it, big guy. Mom seems to like you well enough, and that’s important to me.”

Daniel threw his hands in the air then pushed his glasses up on his nose. “Oh, for goodness’ sake, Sean.” He acted like he’d punch Chase in the gut, causing him to catch his fist in a reflex move. “We think it’s a good move. Can we eat pizza now?”

“Sure. And thanks,” he said as Daniel and Heather went running down the hall. Sean stayed behind to face him man to man. “You got something to say to me?”

“My dad isn’t going to like this,” he voiced flatly.

“I don’t really care,” Chase admitted.

“Me, either. Let’s eat pizza. Oh, you have to propose in front of us. They left that part out.”

“That isn’t very romantic. What if I refuse?”

“Seriously? You know what we’re capable of by now.”

“You’re right. I’ll do it.” The surrender was complete. “After pizza?”

“Definitely after pizza.”

CHAPTER 20

Although Robert didn't show up for the morning services at church, he did arrive promptly at the house to pick up Heather for rehearsal. He didn't have much to say, since Chase was hovering.

"Hungry? We've got plenty of pizza and salad left," he offered the ex. He figured since he would undoubtedly be around for a number of years, he'd better make a peace offering sooner rather than later.

"No thanks. Overslept this morning. Ate a late breakfast. Sorry I missed the program."

Tessa didn't comment, but her evil eye spoke volumes. "You do understand you have to stay for her class's practice then her solo and the daddy-daughter practice. You'll sit outside in the parent area. Grass Valley police will have security in case Gallo shows up to try and snatch Kelly again. They'll call you when it's your turn."

"Got it." He opened the door and relieved Heather of her dance bag. "Ready?"

She took his hand and smiled happily as she pulled him out the door.

Once they were gone, Chase waited until Tessa turned to face him. "You know he's not going to stay the whole time, right?"

"Heather will be hurt." Tessa sighed hopelessly. "Why won't he just see how important these kids are and that he can't expect them to keep forgiving him?"

"I'll go check on the progress with Gallo. I missed a call from Michaels. I'll swing by and sit out in my car in case he bails. Okay?"

"I'm sorry to dump my past life on you." She reached out and took his hand.

"Well, you are a lot to take." He grinned. "I could be globe-trotting, hunting terrorists, and dodging bullets if it weren't for you." He placed his hand on her cheek. "It's going to be okay."

As predicted, after an hour of listening to The Nutcracker music start and stop multiple times, Robert was called on stage for the final practice of the daddy-daughter dance. Tessa texted Chase to say Robert called and had to take care of a problem with one of his clients in North San Juan. Chase was already turning the corner to park the car and quickly entered the performing arts building.

Robert was staring at his phone when he approached. Chase grabbed it out of his hand and looked at the screen. There was a picture of a much younger woman.

"Hey," Robert snapped angrily.

Chase handed the phone back to him. "Client?"

"She was. Said she wanted to talk to me."

"Did you rehearse your part?"

"How is this any of your business?" Robert fumed.

"I'm making it my business. You're a piece of work, you know that? Kids grow up fast, and what you invest now will come back to you tenfold when they grow up."

"So, besides teaching French literature, something no one cares about, you give child development advice."

"Robert, next time you want to know something about me, ask. Don't go behind my back to a fed or try to get rid of me." He patted Robert's chest before withdrawing. "Who knows. You might end up riding in a van, blindfolded, to an undisclosed place to be interrogated." Which Chase had done to him several years earlier.

"I guess I can't trust the FBI after all if he told you about my unfortunate run-in with a bunch of criminals."

The inclination to throw Robert up against the wall and hold him there by the neck was tempting him more than he could stand. Instead, he walked away and found a seat near the door.

Robert gave a "humph" followed by a snide smile as if he'd won an argument. It probably was a good thing the man didn't know what he was capable of.

He read a book on his phone while he waited an hour for Heather to finish. She froze when he stood and searched the area as if trying to find her dad.

"Something came up, baby cakes. Hope it's okay I came. I thought maybe we could meet the boys and your mom for ice cream."

The fact she didn't comment on her father's absence or ask why bothered him a little. Instead of being a nonstop chatterbox, she didn't say a word, only stared out the car window. Were her feelings hurt, or was she tired from the rehearsal? He tried to fill in the gaps of silence as they drove to Scoops, their favorite ice cream parlor.

Once home, the kids huddled up again and pushed him toward their mom then motioned to him behind her back. They mimicked getting on one knee to Heather when Tessa walked out of the room. The plan had been to propose after lunch, but Robert showed up sooner than expected. There had been a secret meeting where the kids let him know he had to wait until later.

"Okay. Okay. Okay," he mumbled quietly. "Here she comes."

"What's going on?" She joined them in front of the Christmas tree.

"Hmm. I wanted to ask you something, Tessa, about us." Chase reached to hold her hand.

Heather returned to her bubbly self and began jumping up and down. "He wants to…"

Sean Patrick grabbed her back in his arms as Daniel covered her mouth with his hand.

Tessa glanced at the kids then at Chase. "Ask me what?"

Chase reached under the tree to retrieve a small velvet box before going down on one knee. "Tessa, I love you more than I can ever tell you. I want to try and show you for the rest of our lives. Will you marry me?"

Although she knew it was coming—eventually, she burst into

tears and let him slip the diamond ring onto her finger. "Yes. A thousand times yes."

The three kids ran forward and hugged their mother as Chase pulled her into his arms and kissed her without fear he'd be found out. After the kids were tucked in and fast asleep, they finally had time to savor their life together.

~~~~

Anthony Gallo discovered Horace had been arrested by listening to the news. The man was weak, but it was unlikely he'd tell them anything concerning the plan to escape to Mexico. There were plenty of people who could seek revenge on his behalf if the man decided to betray him. Thanks to the bumbling idiot, he knew his daughter, Kelly, would be participating in a dance recital. At least Horace, even with his shortcomings, had thought to get a schedule of the child's weekly activities, places the family frequented, and special events, like the dance recital.

He had ditched the car used in his escape from the church. That other little girl who helped foil his getaway must be the best friend Horace told him about. Now he thought maybe taking her, too, would keep Kelly calm. He didn't want a crying kid alerting people on his trip south.

After dumping the car near the small town of Rough and Ready, about a half hour from Grass Valley, Gallo found the replacement Horace had secured for him at a truck stop. He bought a shaving kit and shower time to remove several days of grime. With the addition of clean clothes, he ditched the Santa suit. Since his long coat had covered it, no one paid much attention to him. After gathering a few supplies he'd need for the trip south, which included a teddy bear and juice packs, he added a blanket and a neck pillow. Since he didn't completely trust Horace to keep his mouth shut, he drove back toward Grass Valley and pulled off onto a gravel road where he could get a few hours' sleep before heading out again. According to the radio, police were searching for him. Maybe with his respectable appearance, clean sedan, and taking extra care not to break any speed limits, he'd be fine.

He'd purchased a couple of burner phones and stored them in the console for later if he needed them. Horace had placed several
~~~~

magazines of ammo in the trunk with other supplies in case he had to hike out of a tight spot. But, for now, he wanted his kid.

He also wanted to take care of Deacon once and for all. The only reason his daughter had agreed to go with him was the promise to hurt her dad if she didn't. He believed she loved him. Maybe she did for a while. Guess the old man had a lot to do with her ratting him out and being sent to jail. Taking the kid would show both of them who was in charge.

Turning his thoughts to the other little girl gave him pause. Whatever she hit him with was hard, making him drop Kelly and roll down the hill. That kid wouldn't be a pushover. Maybe he would need to restrain her. As his eyes began to droop into sleep, he ran the possibilities through his plan of escape until he was too tired to continue.

~~~~

The following day, the weather turned beautiful with the sun shining bright and reflecting off what was left of the snowfall. Since school was out until after New Year's, the kids took advantage of their free time to play in the snow. The neighborhood kids knew if they played at their house, Tessa would be serving hot chocolate and cookies and she did not disappoint.

The Ervins who lived next door and also worked for Enigma came over to keep an eye on the kids, along with helping to wrap a few more presents for under the tree. Chase felt confident the three of them would keep a close eye on the comings and goings of strange cars in the neighborhood. He was more concerned about Kelly Parker than the home front. Officer Michaels had an officer cruising through every hour. Mr. Parker had the police on speed dial. They kept Kelly inside, much to her disappointment, knowing her best friend down the street was playing in the snow without her.

"Any news of Gallo?" Chase asked when he took Michaels out to lunch.

"Found a car outside Rough and Ready at an abandoned storefront. It was a rental. Guess whose name it was under?"

"Horace, the insurance guy."

"Yep. Special Agent Martin had a team there doing forensics
~~~~

in no time, but they came up with nothing as to who left it there. That was an easy trace after he admitted to it. The interesting thing is he rented a second one a week ago and left it at a truck stop in Rough and Ready. No trace of it according to your agent friend. Showed a picture around of Gallo and no one recognized him. However, they did remember a car being parked out there for several days. Speculation is he was there during the night shift. Going to check back to see if anyone saw him."

"Horace give any indication where he might be headed?"

"He couldn't stop talking. Said we had to protect him, though, because Gallo has a lot of friends who would hurt him if he gave anything away. Gallo plans to head to Mexico and was going to take Kelly with him. Already has a job with one of the cartels down there."

"Great father he'll make." Chase held his cup for the waitress to pour him more coffee before he continued. "Tonight is the recital Kelly will be in. Any chance Gallo knows about that?"

"Unfortunately, yes. Horace gave him a list of places he thought the Parkers would be over Christmas. Since he carries their insurance, he knows a lot about them, and it was easy trying to act interested in their daily life."

"What's going to become of him?"

"Turning him over to the feds. Not sure after that. We don't get high-profile cases here in Grass Valley. And I don't want any more. There's been more excitement in the last couple of days than we've had all year. If I wanted this kind of trouble, I'd have stayed in Sacramento."

"Maybe Gallo is long gone. He could be almost to Mexico by now."

"Good thing Heather clobbered him with that rock. We might be talking about something entirely different right now if she hadn't."

Chase sighed and grabbed the check. "I gotta get back home. Tessa is making a special dinner for Heather since she is the Sugar Plum Fairy tonight. She's been quiet today. Not sure if it's recital jitters or the kidnapping. She didn't sleep well last night."

"I'll stop by when I get off duty to make sure things are secure. We're stretched pretty thin."

"Agent Martin promised he'd be around with a couple of his

guys. The rest are still hunting Gallo. I'll be there, too." He shook the officer's hand. "Thanks for all you do. You guys don't get enough credit."

There was enough muddy snow slush on his car that Gallo didn't worry the police officer and Mr. Muscles might spot him. Most likely, a description about the car was circulating by now. He'd managed to purchase a few stickers. One was a Santa and a bunch of elves representing a family, for the back window. The second sticker he bought was one for the bumper that bragged about his honor roll student. And, finally, the last one was Thank a Veteran. Inwardly, he thought he was freaking Mr. America.

Watching them walk down the street toward their vehicles, Gallo decided this might not be so hard after all. Those two dummies should have spotted him right away. He carefully pulled away from the curb and went to find a new hiding place until the program tonight.

CHAPTER 21

"Where is he?" Tessa fumed quietly where only Chase could hear her. "The boys just texted me that Robert is still not here. When I left Heather in the back with a couple of stage moms, she was nervous. I'm not sure if it was because her father wasn't here and might miss her performance or not show for the daddy-daughter dance."

Chase pulled out the tickets for the show and handed them to her. "Go get the boys and find their seats. Have them save the other three for us in case he shows up." He laid his hand on her arm. "We're here. She'll be happy about that. I'm going backstage to check things out and give her a pep talk. Is that okay with you?"

Tessa sighed. "You're amazing."

"Heather thinks I'm full of baloney."

"Amazing baloney."

"You always know the right things to say," he moaned. "I'm going to put on my Dr. Phil hat. Wish me luck."

"Oh my gosh. Have you been watching Dr. Phil?" Tessa choked on her words.

"I read several of his books. I didn't want to end up on his show in the future because I screwed up our family. Thought I'd better get help."

Tessa covered her mouth to keep from bursting into laughter. "Go before I lose it."

He smirked mischievously and watched her head for the entrance where people were waiting to get in.

Chase ran into Agent Martin backstage talking to several other agents and a police officer. From his stance and solemn face, he guessed the man was giving them a few orders and updates. One officer would be at the front door, another two at the back. He would be on the move to spot for areas not as secure or suspicious activity.

Agent Martin glanced his way and gave him a greeting with a chin up. He limped slightly, but, knowing the agent, he wouldn't let that stop him if push came to shove where Gallo was concerned. "We think Gallo is back in town. He tried to reach Horace with a burner phone. We couldn't trace it."

"What did he say?" Chase asked.

"To meet him on the edge of town at nine tonight. But according to Horace, that wasn't part of the original plan. He thinks it's a distraction and that we have Horace's phone bugged. We'll have state troopers at both ends of town, just in case."

"I need to check on Heather. She may have a little stage fright."

"I saw her over there. She was talking to the custodian a bit ago."

"Custodian?"

"I checked him out. Some old guy with gray hair and bushy eyebrows. I was standing right there, Chase."

"Okay. Okay. I got a bad feeling is all."

He walked off and noticed what appeared to be a custodian in a blue jumpsuit with the name of the theater on his back. He swept an already clean floor. He'd wanted to check the guy out again to reassure himself. The problem with PTSD was you never got over looking for the enemy.

Then he spotted Heather, reminiscent of a little girl from a Degas painting. Tessa had waited to dress her once they arrived. Now she was all sparkly with makeup and her hair in banana curls. She began stretching to loosen up, followed by a lot of toe pointing. The other little girls were doing the same in their ruffled dresses the color of pineapple.

"Excuse me." He pretended to be confused. "I'm looking for Heather Scott. Have you seen her?"

Heather smiled the biggest smile he'd ever seen. "It's me, Chasey!"

"Oh, my goodness. It is," he said, putting his hands on his cheeks. "Where did that little ugly duckling go? You are so beautiful."

"I know you don't think I'm an ugly duckling. You're just saying that."

He pulled up a chair and got eye to eye with her. "You're right. You are the most beautiful girl here, even without all that makeup." He held out his hands, and she slipped her tiny ones inside before tilting her head. "I'm excited to see you dance. This is my first dance recital."

"Really?" she asked. "You should get out more."

"You're probably right. Are you nervous?"

She bit her bottom lip and shrugged. "Maybe a little."

"That's a good thing. When your brain and body feel like that, it sparks a big gush of blood to your muscles and heart. So, you'll probably be so fantastic out there, you'll have a talent agent waiting for you after the show."

"That sounds like more baloney, but thanks for making me feel better." She stepped into his embrace. "I'm glad you came." She began a nervous pat on his forearms. "I have three dances. The first one is the song from The Nutcracker party scene, and that is my ballet class. Then, later, I get to be the Sugar Plum Fairy. I'm doing it alone. Like, all by myself."

"You must be pretty good." He couldn't help but be amused by her eyes shining with excitement. "And the last one? Oh, wait. Is that the daddy-daughter dance?"

She bobbed her head then stared down at his hands and rubbed them tenderly. "Yep."

"Are you worried about that?"

Another shrug. "I guess. You know my dad said he didn't like he might have to wear a pink boa or a funny tutu around his waist. Said it wasn't manly. I don't know what that means, but I think he just doesn't want to dance with me."

"What I heard was he found out how good I was at dancing

with you, and he was afraid he'd look silly and embarrass you. He's kind of a klutz, I think." He watched her bottom lip protrude in skepticism as her eyes narrowed. "So, maybe, if he gets stage fright, do you think I could dance with you?"

"Of course," she said happily. "That would work."

"Well, if you're sure." He was relieved she didn't exhibit anxiety over the kidnapping attempt. Time would tell whether that returned to haunt her.

"It's always good to have a backup plan." She backed out of his embrace. "I'd better go. It's almost time."

Chase stood up and stared at her, trying to remain tough in spite of all the glitter, pink stuff, and smell of hair spray. "Your mom will be back to help you change for your next number." He dusted white powder off the arm of her costume. "What's this?" He smelled it. "Smells like baby powder."

Heather finished dusting it off. "Oh, it fell out of the custodian's head. I thought it was a dandruff problem. I didn't want him to be embarrassed so I pretended not to notice."

"Why were you talking to him?"

"Oh, he wanted to know about the dances and who my best friend was—weird stuff. But I was polite. I promise. He was old. You're kinda old, and I would want others to be kind to you, Chasey."

"Jeez. Thanks."

"Sure." She hurried to join her friends. Little Kelly ran to her, and they gave each other hugs.

He backed away slowly until he saw two instructors taking charge of the dancers. With a quick pivot, he started prowling the other areas of the building in search of the custodian. Then he ran into Agent Martin.

"Gallo is here," he growled. "He's the custodian, disguised as an older man. He's been asking questions about Kelly."

Agent Martin touched his earwig and gave orders to be on the lookout for Gallo in disguise. Both men combed the area, but Gallo was nowhere to be found.

"He may have spotted you from the church." Agent Martin continued to turn his head, scanning for Gallo. "Go sit with your family." The agent held up his hand when Chase opened his mouth to refuse. "Both girls are up first. I'm right here and won't move until she exits the stage and you've come back. Bring Tessa. Nothing scarier than a pissed-off mom when it comes to their kid. And we both know Tessa is way past that after being with Enigma these past few years. She's capable of protecting them."

Chase agreed and hurried to find his seat. He whispered the problem in Tessa's ear. "Dennis is offstage looking like a pit bull that hasn't eaten in a few days. Just enjoy this first routine. I'm going to speak to Sean Patrick so he'll stay vigilant."

"What about the Parkers?"

"Well, he's on crutches and has no business playing the hero. Casually suggest Deacon come backstage with you until the daddy-daughter dance. He's filling in since Kelly has practiced so hard. You be the judge of how much to tell him. After this first dance, I'm going back, too. Hopefully, Robert will be here by then."

The first dance was longer than Chase expected, and he felt himself being too distracted by Heather's dancing. Everything she did distracted him, it seemed. Fatherhood wasn't going to be a piece of cake.

The upside was Sean Patrick didn't ask him twenty questions, just said "Cool, got this, dude," then turned his head around like a possessed owl. A thumbs-up was what he got, and a high five. Progress.

After the first dance, Chase slipped out and backstage where the dancers were being herded into a large room. It was off-limits to dads, since the girls were changing into other outfits for their routine. He waited outside the door and felt like a bouncer with no sense of humor since Agent Martin had begun his search for Gallo. Once Tessa arrived, he took a deep breath of relief.

"Robert show up?"

"Just now. Saw him out in the foyer, talking on his phone. I left him, thinking, surely, he'd go inside after I shoved a program in his hand and underlined when Heather would do her solo. He waved me off, so here I am. Heather's in there, I'm guessing."

"Of course, I'm a one-eyed cyclops and can't go inside," Chase moaned. "Women."

"You're not strong enough to go in there. Trust me." She patted his chest, drawing a reluctant smile. "I have my trusty Taser in my pocket if needed. I would hate to use it and blow my image of a sweet mom who bakes cookies."

"I think you're overthinking how people see you." He ran his hand down the side of her blazer until he felt the Taser. "Is there another way into this room?"

"Yes. I'll stay near that door if you're going to be here."

"I'm going to go back and forth to the stage entrance since Officer Michaels just came in the back door. I see Dennis waving at me and frowning. I'll be able to check on the boys that way. Michaels will probably be along here, too."

"Sounds good." She sighed and started to open the door.

"We're going to get him."

"I know."

~~~~

Tessa received a hug from Heather when she joined the chaos. Before she could respond to watching her dance, Heather ran over to a group of girls where Kelly was playing a game. The girls didn't appear to have a care in the world. The dance studio owner took advantage of an extra pair of hands, and she quickly found herself re-pinning hair, fixing makeup, or adjusting bows on several girls.

When a game of London Bridge started near the back exit door, Tessa repositioned herself closer. She noticed the door was cracked open about two inches. As she took a step in that direction, she detected movement. Pushing the door open, all she saw was one of the moms coming out of the restroom.

"Sorry I took so long to come help. One of my other girls was in the second performance," the mom said.

"No problem." Tessa smiled with a bit of relief. She pulled the door shut, but there was no way to lock it.

The chaos continued with the volume turned on high. There were dance instructors clapping their hands to this group or that. Like obedient sheep seeing their shepherd, each group calmed down and sat at the feet of the instructors to hear last-minute instructions. Three more groups of girls disappeared to perform then returned before it was intermission. She sent Chase a text that said So far, so good.
~~~~

~ ~ ~ ~

Chase cornered Robert talking on the phone and waited for him to stop his legal prattle, followed by yes, yes, no, of course, whatever and you don't say. Chase finally grabbed the phone and disconnected it before tossing it in the trash.

"What are you doing? That was an important client."

"More important than dancing the daddy-daughter dance with Heather?"

"In this instance, yes. This is a big case for me, and I'm not going to blow it. She'll understand. Tell her I'm not coming to do the daddy-daughter thing. This might take a few minutes. You're pretty light on your feet." He smirked. "You do it."

"You should be ashamed of yourself."

"I don't need you to tell me what to do concerning my kids." He fished the phone out of the trash and redialed. "Sorry about that," he said with a chuckle. "You were saying?"

Chase stormed away and headed backstage. The dance school owner made a call for the daddy-daughter dance fathers to make their way to their assigned waiting area. It would be their turn in a few minutes. He quickly joined them, and a slow appreciative applause floated across the audience for the brave fathers prepared to expose their lack of dance skills.

It was then he noticed off-duty police officers running up the stage steps and disappearing behind the curtains. There were screams and then crashes as he pushed ahead of the other dads who already wore deer-in-the-headlight expressions.

Little girls and teachers were huddled in the dim light of the backstage area. Deacon had Kelly and Heather by the hand. He was saying. "It's okay. No worries, ladies. No problem. It's all being taken care of. Right, girls?"

CHAPTER 22

"Mommy, I have to go to the restroom?" Heather had her knees locked together and was chewing on her bottom lip.

"Oh dear. Okay. There's a restroom right outside the door. Let's take Kelly, too."

"Okay." Kelly smiled sweetly and gave Tessa a hug around her waist.

It was a tiny restroom. Tessa could imagine her mother saying it wasn't big enough to cuss a cat. But they managed to not pee on themselves or their outfits.

Once they joined the others, Tessa quickly fixed Heather's hair in a bun and gave it a heavy dose of hair spray. Kelly wanted hers styled the same way, so she fixed hers as well.

"That creepy janitor is not supposed to be here where us girls are." Kelly nodded in an all-knowing way.

"I know, sweetheart," Tessa said absentmindedly as she examined Heather's hairdo.

"Then why is he standing behind you?" Kelly asked innocently.

Tessa jerked around to see Gallo standing three feet away from her and the girls. "Run," she shouted.

The teachers, having been informed of the security risks,

threw open the door at the other end of the room and tried to herd the girls out.

"Run," Tessa repeated to Heather.

Before Tessa could see if they obeyed, Gallo lunged at her and grabbed the lapel of her jacket. With hair spray still in hand, she unloaded it at full force into his eyes, causing him to release her and let out an anguished cry. He staggered back, rubbing the hair spray away and shaking his head. Before he could recover, Tessa charged him and hit him in the nose with the fatty part of her palm, sending blood running down his face. Yet he was able to open his wounded eyes and glare at her as he touched his nose. A growl came from his mouth as he once more moved toward her. Tessa didn't choose flight but to fight instead. When he closed in, she grabbed his shirt, yanking him to her then rammed her knee into his groin. A painful yelp bent him over so that she locked her hands together in a double fist, bringing it down on the back of his neck. When he collapsed on the floor, moaning, she took out her Taser and fired it at him.

Agent Martin and several of his agents, plus Chase and Officer Michaels swarmed into the room. She glanced behind her to see if Heather and Kelly had made it out. The thought of them seeing her take down a criminal was unsettling.

Several agents had him cuffed and on his feet in seconds. Gallo tried to shake them off, but his feeble attempts subsided when Tessa stepped toward him. He cowered enough to make her husband grin.

"Don't mess with my kids," she warned with a sneer.

"Did you need to tase me? I was down," he complained.

"You tased him?" Agent Martin inquired with a smirk on his face. "Was that necessary?"

"No. But I hadn't tried it out yet and, since it was charged and ready to go"—she shrugged—"I thought, why not?"

"I'm going to pretend I didn't hear that," Officer Michaels announced.

The other men laughed and told her if she ever needed a job to let them know.

The owner of the dance studio made a quick announcement about why the police were present and that there had been a breach. Officer Michaels, who everyone seemed to know, reassured the crowd things were under control and that, with the help of the FBI, they had apprehended a dangerous felon hiding in the building. He'd showed little resistance. All the children were safe and a quick-thinking mom had gotten them out of harm's way immediately. Applause filled the theater until the officer held up his hand for silence.

The owner of the studio thanked law enforcement and then suggested the show continue.

~~~~

Tessa was kneeling in front of Heather who had her head bowed and bottom lip stuck out so far, there was a good chance she'd trip over it during the next dance number.

"What seems to be the problem?" Chase asked.

"My daddy didn't come to see me be the Sugar Plum Fairy. He promised. I'm up next."

"I think I saw your daddy outside during intermission. He's probably looking for your brothers."

"Really?" She beamed.

"Yes. He said he was very excited to see you do your special dance."

Heather motioned for him to bend down. He obeyed and let her little arms circle his neck. Lifting her up, he felt her soft lips kiss his cheek. She whispered in his ear, "I wish you were my daddy."

He hugged her. "Me, too, sweet girl. Me, too." He kissed her on the temple, stopping when she jerked back and frowned. "What?"

The little girl huffed and wiggled enough he was forced to set her feet on the floor. "Chasey, you're going to mess up my makeup. Men," she said, shoving her hands on her hips. "Is my crown straight?"

"Women. You're all alike." He chuckled. "Your crown is perfect."

"Better get over there, sweetheart. They're lining up to go on stage." Tessa fluffed her tutu, checked the crown, and gave her a thumbs-up. As she ran to join the other Nutcracker characters, Tessa smiled then stood with his help. "Is Robert really here?"
~~~~

"Talking to a client. Told me to mind my own business."

"After all she's been through in the last few days, if he doesn't do this daddy-daughter dance, it will break her heart."

"That's not going to happen."

She frowned. "You can't hurt him here in front of the whole town, Chase. Or anywhere else, either."

"I hate that guy. What is he thinking?"

Tessa bit her bottom lip and blinked hard, her eyes shiny. "He takes things for granted. Because he's their father, he believes he'll always be the one they prefer." She laid a gentle hand on his forearm. "I love the way you are with the kids. I know they give you a hard time, but they do care about you, especially Heather."

He took a deep breath at hearing those words and moved to the area where parents could watch without returning to their seats. Several dads stood there grinning like they'd won the lottery as the music began.

"I don't know one thing about all this stuff, but they sure are cute," one balding dad said.

"I nearly had a heart attack when my wife told me how much this was costing us. Now I get it," another dad joined in and added a chuckle. "Worth every penny."

They looked at Chase who had folded his arms across his chest.

"What about you? Which one is yours?" one of the dads asked Chase.

Chase grinned and pointed toward Heather who was taking her place in center stage. "The Sugar Plum Fairy."

There was a lot of grinning and awes as the curtain slid back.

Tchaikovsky's "Dance of the Sugar Plum Fairy" began, and Chase felt both pride and anxiety at knowing Heather had the lead. What if she fell? Would it be appropriate to go get her? Would he have to bust a few heads if these dads laughed at her? But then she started to dance. His heart beat so hard, he could barely breathe. Heather twirled, tiptoed, leaped, and did the dance perfectly. When she bowed, the applause was loud and long. She turned into the little girl he knew at that point and jumped up and down, waving to someone in the audience. Chase leaned to the side and saw Robert taking a seat. Hopefully, Heather didn't realize that he'd just come in. She probably thought he was giving her a standing ovation.

Then she was running toward Chase and Tessa, all smiles and sparkles.

"Mommy, was I good?"

"Sensational!" She pulled her close. "I'm so proud of you and the hard work you put into that dance."

Heather tilted her head toward Chase and batted her eyes like Tessa always did, except for her it wasn't a nervous tick. It was pure manipulation. "Well?"

He went down on one knee and smiled, his emotions and reasonable thinking skills melting so fast he wasn't sure he could speak without choking up. "You were great. I think I might want to take ballet myself."

A giggle escaped her pretty red lips, and she threw her arms around his neck and hugged so tight he nearly lost his balance. "You can kiss me now, Chasey."

And he did, on her cheek, hair-sprayed hair, and neck. "You were amazing."

"I know! Right?"

Next came the teenagers who filed out to do "The Waltz of the Flowers." Heather stood in front of Chase, holding both of his hands, even after all the little girls ran back to find their mothers or check their makeup. The main ballerina in the number had Heather mesmerized until she gazed up at Chase.

"I'm gonna be her one of these days. I want to dance like that."

Tessa rubbed his back as she laid her head against his shoulder. "I'm so happy," she whispered.

"Me, too." He kissed her hair and basked in the feeling of holding hands with his little angel.

Tessa helped the dads maneuver the pink tutus around their waists. They took it in stride because their daughters were eating it up. The dads pretended to dance with each other and acted silly for their daughters. When Chase walked out with his tutu on, she didn't know whether to laugh or cry. The man was a battle-hardened soldier who had been to hell and back. Yet he sacrificed his manly pride to make a little girl happy.

"Doesn't he look cute?" Heather called to Kelly as she held his hand and wore the boa that would, at a certain point, end up on his neck.

The teacher stepped out on stage to announce the last dance of the night. She told the audience how proud she was of the fathers who stepped up and tried to be a part of their class. The music began, and the dads walked out onto the stage. The girls, all ages, twirled their way to their perspective dads and began the routine. During certain parts of the routine, dads lifted their little feet off the floor and spun around in a show of talent and grace. It ended as quickly as it began. The dads took a bow with their daughters and left the stage to wild applause. Parents were to pick up their children in the side lobby.

Tessa and Chase stood talking to Deacon as their girls giggled and bragged on their partners. Soon, the Parkers were backstage and praised the daddy-daughter dancers. They brought Kelly flowers as was customary then took pictures at the backdrop provided by the dance school.

"Did you bring—" Chase whispered to Tessa.

She handed him a bag. He removed a bouquet of wildflowers in all the colors of the rainbow.

"For me?" Heather chirped. "They're beautiful." She tried to smell them, followed by a sneeze. "Come on. Let's have our picture taken."

Robert and the boys showed up and bragged on her skills. Sean Patrick gave Chase a condescending smile and a fist bump to the arm. "Way to go, big guy. I guess even knights in shining armor need to learn to dance."

"Yeah. Maybe we should change your name from Silent Knight from a few years ago to Twinkle Toes Knight." Daniel fist-bumped Chase's gut before he burst out laughing.

"Very funny." Chase gave them both a playful shove.

Robert picked up Heather and kissed her. "You were so pretty. I loved your dance. I missed your first dance because I was bringing a surprise."

"Surprise?" Heather asked as he set her feet on the floor.

"Yep. The car dealership up at Truckee drove the new van down for us. I had to wait. Let's go get some ice cream." He clapped his hands together. "I mean, if your mom doesn't care. Did you have plans, Tessa?"

"I guess not. It's been a long day. Don't be too late."

"No school tomorrow. A little later shouldn't be a problem. Right guys?" Robert chuckled as he fanned his hand out at the kids.

Heather took Chase's hand and stared up at him. "Want to go?"

"I think your dad wants to have special time with you kids." Chase pinched her cheek.

Sean Patrick watched Heather then refocused on his father before addressing Chase. "Come on, big guy. But you're going to have to take the boa off. It's really embarrassing."

Chase pulled off the boa and wrapped it around Sean Patrick's neck and quickly took a picture on his phone. "Now, if you start that Twinkle Toes nonsense, I'll just pull out my picture of you."

The boys rushed at Chase as he wrapped his arms around them and pretended to block their punches. An expression of shock covered Robert's face. Did he see the tides of respect had shifted in Chase's favor?

"Well, that would be fine if you and Tessa want to come with us." Robert sounded hesitant, but Chase figured it had dawned on him what he was losing.

"I think ice cream would be a great idea. Besides, Tessa and I want to talk to you about something."

Heather took her mother's and Chase's hands, swinging them back and forth. "We have a surprise, too."

"We sure do, Bobby, I mean Robert." Chase winked at the boys. "Right, boys?"

Sean Patrick smirked. "This should be good."

The family made their way outside as the strobe lights of police cars were leaving the performing arts building. Officer Michaels tipped his hat to the group as Agent Dennis Martin smiled at them without saying a word.

Once more, Chase became aware of how his life had changed in a few short years. And soon, surrounded by family and friends, he would marry Tessa again, this time to make it official for the world to know. This new life had become an adventure he hadn't expected.

The End

ABOUT THE AUTHOR

Besides serving as a Solar System Ambassador for NASA's Jet Propulsion Lab, and attending Space Camp for Educators, Tierney served as a Geo-teacher for National Geographic. Her love of travel and cultures took her on adventures throughout Africa, Asia and Europe. From the Great Wall of China to floating the Okavango Delta of Botswana, Tierney weaves her unique experiences into the adventures she loves to write. Living on a Native American reservation and in a mining town, fuels the characters in the Enigma and Dark Side series.

Being a lifelong educator, she also helps beginning writers in their quest to becoming a published author through her workshops and classes. She is often asked to speak at writer conferences and community events. Now with twenty-three books under her belt, plus audiobooks, Tierney began searching for a new idea to engage readers and writers alike.

Tierney discovered another creative outlet when she learned how to make journals and notebooks. Turning simple details and pictures into beautiful keepsakes for memories, scrapbook ideas, story concepts and travel adventures, became another passion for this busy full-time writer. She uses the pen name Louiza Pearl in honor of her grandmothers. Besides writing and publishing action/adventure, military romance, supernatural and geopolitical thriller books, Tierney has added a fun way to write down your own dreams for the future. Find her at tierneyjames.com or on Amazon.

Other Publications by Tierney James

The Enigma Series Vol. 1-10

The Hemlock Switch
Martyrs Never Die
Invisible Goodbye
The Knight Before Chaos
Black Mamba
Kifaru
Rooftop Angels
The Winds of Deception
An Unlikely Hero

Lipstick & Danger Series

House of Miracles
The Rescued Heart

The Dark Side Series

Dark Side of Noon
Dark Side of Morning

Stand Alone Books

Dance of the Devil's Trill
Turnback Creek
Lipstick & Danger – A Collection of Short Stories When Escape is Your Only Option
Lipstick & Danger – Recipes to Die For

Other

How to Market a Book Someone Besides Your Mother Will Read
There's a Superhero in the Library
Zombie Meatloaf
Mission K-9 Rescue
African Safari: A Thematic Lesson Book for Teachers

Milton Keynes UK
Ingram Content Group UK Ltd.
UKHW022126051124
450708UK00015B/1205

9 781965 460283